BROKEN SOULS

A BROKEN REBEL BROTHERHOOD NOVEL

ANDI RHODES

Copyright © 2020 by ANDI RHODES

All rights reserved.

No part of this book may be reproduced in any form or by any electronic or mechanical means, including information storage and retrieval systems, without written permission from the author, except for the use of brief quotations in a book review.

Cover Artwork – © 2020 L.J. Anderson of Mayhem Cover Creations

For my husband, Andy, who has supported me and loved me through this crazy journey.

ALSO BY ANDI RHODES

Broken Rebel Brotherhood

Broken Souls

Broken Innocence

Broken Boundaries

Broken Rebel Brotherhood: Complete Series Box set

Broken Rebel Brotherhood: Next Generation

Broken Hearts

Broken Wings

Broken Mind

Bastards and Badges

Stark Revenge

Slade's Fall

Jett's Guard

Soulless Kings MC

Fender

Joker

Piston

Greaser

Riker

Trainwreck

Squirrel

Gibson

Satan's Legacy MC

Snow's Angel

Toga's Demons

Magic's Torment

You deserve:
Laughter and love,
sweetness and desire,
dreams that turn
into reality,
and become the color
of your eyes.

~ Mark Anthony

1

SADIE

Holy shit! Every inch of me screamed in agony. I knew I had to block out the pain if I had a chance in hell of escaping. I had to get away. Lying on the living room floor, I lifted my head to track Ian's movements. I was grateful that my eyes weren't swelling shut, as I knew that I'd likely have to drive if I was going to flee. My vision blurred red, but I could still see. Ian was pacing back and forth, leaving bloody footprints on the hardwood floor. My blood.

Ian had been pissed off before he even walked in the door. Something about the takeover of another dealership not going as planned. There was no "hello" when he came home. Not that there ever was anymore. There was no warning. He had just laid into me. It had started out as just yelling, but apparently, I'd lost my mind and yelled back. Wrong move. I hadn't yelled back in so long, and it had felt so damn good.

That feeling didn't last long, though.

Steel-toe boots entered my line of vision and the next thing I knew, Ian had drawn his leg back and kicked me on the side of the head. My ears rang and my vision blurred but I managed to hold onto consciousness. Barely.

"St...stop...pl...please." I hated showing weakness, but I pleaded anyway. To no avail. His size elevens rammed my side next. Pain exploded in my ribcage and the sound of crunching bone reached my ears. A gasp rushed over my lips, followed by a groan.

"Shut up, bitch!" Ian raged.

It had never been this bad before. He wasn't trying to hide where the damage was this time, so I knew I'd reached the end. He was going to kill me. His boots receded from my line of sight, and as I gingerly lifted my head, I noted that he was stalking toward the kitchen. Ian had a thing for knives, so my fear shot up a notch. Or ten. When he was really angry, knives were his way of taunting me. He'd never cut me before, but he would this time. I knew my time was up.

Something in me snapped and I knew it was now or never. I had to muster the strength to stand. I did so, swaying and almost passing out. Bracing myself on the back of the couch, I took several torturous breaths. Once I felt confident that I wouldn't fall over, I darted for the door. We lived in a large house and I knew Ian wouldn't hear my escape right away. But the second he came back in the living room, my reprieve would be over. I had to get out. Pain like I had never experienced made it almost impossible, but my desire to live won out.

I ran!

I sprinted as fast as I ever had, tree branches slapping me in the face as I wound my way through the dense woods behind our house. Ian and I had been married for four years and together for six. I'd known Ian McCord for what felt like my entire life, but really it was only eight years. I had been one of society's invisibles. A homeless teen just trying to survive. For the most part, I'd had a roof over my head, clothes on my back and food in my stomach, but I had never had a home. Not until I was sixteen, and that had only lasted a year. Then I'd met Ian at nineteen and thought I was dreaming because he paid attention to me more than anyone had in two years.

Keep running, I told myself. The past is just that. The past. Keep running. I had practiced this run so many times while Ian had been at work. I had wanted to know the route like I knew the freckles across my face. I hadn't planned on the intense throbbing of my injuries, but I was a fighter. At least from this day forward. Tripping over fallen limbs and sliding on wet leaves, it was taking longer than I'd hoped but I knew the car couldn't be that much farther. I'd hidden it, out of necessity, because Ian didn't let me have a vehicle. It was hidden in a copse of trees, where he'd never find it. Ian was not the woodsy type, so it hadn't been too difficult to hide.

"Fucking bitch!" Ian yelled as he ran after me. "You can't run far enough to save yourself!" I pictured the spit flying from his mouth as he screamed. The sweat that was inevitably pouring down his face. He wouldn't stop until he found me and killed me. I knew that. But I had to try.

I chanced a glance over my shoulder, toward his voice, which caused me to trip. I reached my hands out to catch myself, moaning when pain shot up my arms at the jolt. My head barely missed hitting the ground, thank fuck, because I knew another blow to my skull would halt my progress and I'd be dead.

It was so dark. My memory was the only thing guiding me to that car. My memory and sheer will. This was the one time the darkness was my friend because Ian didn't know these woods like I did. I hated the dark, but damn, it swept over me like a calming blanket in that moment. My mind started to wander again.

There! The glint of metal caught my eye, and I knew that I was almost free. I could still hear Ian, but I blocked him out. When I got to the car, a little run-down Ford Focus with more rust than metal, I yanked the door open and grabbed the key from the visor. My hands shook as I put the key in the ignition and prayed. I stopped praying so long ago, because let's face it, God stopped listening. But I prayed now. I prayed hard. The car had been sitting for a while, so I hoped it would start. I turned the key and nothing. Shit. Shit, shit, shit. This couldn't be happening. I turned the key again and God must have tuned back in because the car started. I hit the gas, fishtailing as the tires gained purchase, and I got the fuck out of Dodge.

Five hours later...

I was so tired. I stopped at a rest area knowing that I had to try to clean myself up and catch some shut eye. I pulled into a spot at the farthest end of the lot and winced as I reached into the backseat for a hoodie. I had put a few changes of clothes in the car because I'd known I wouldn't be taking a suitcase when I left. Careful not to irritate my injuries further, I pulled the hoodie over my head and pulled the hood down low, almost covering my eyes. There were other cars in the lot and I didn't want to give anyone the opportunity to see me.

For a split second I contemplated asking someone for help but decided against it. I didn't want to chance the cops being called. They hadn't believed me in the past and I didn't know how far Ian's influence reached.

As I made my way to the bathroom, I didn't pass another soul, so I was surprised to see two women at the sinks when I entered. Barely acknowledging them, I turned around and quickly made my way into the family restroom. At least I could have some privacy. The nausea was almost unbearable, and I managed to make it to the toilet before emptying the contents of my stomach. Which wasn't much.

I quickly rinsed my mouth out, swishing water back and forth before spitting it down the drain. I managed to avoid the mirror altogether. I wasn't ready to face how I looked. I didn't even waste time on cleaning my numerous injuries. I needed sleep more than I needed to be clean. After rinsing my mouth a few more times, I walked out of the restroom and returned to my car.

I desperately needed to sleep but that wasn't happening. The darkness was no longer my friend. I couldn't get comfortable because every single inch of me screamed in pain, and I was scared. The memory of Ian's boot crashing into my skull was emblazoned on my brain and the sound of my ribs cracking echoed in my ears. I knew I hadn't driven far enough to be completely free, so I started the car and began to put more distance between me and my past.

As I drove, the aches and pains worsened, and I struggled to keep the blackness at bay. I cranked up the volume on the meager stereo to keep me awake. It made my head pound harder, but I didn't dare turn it down because it was the reminder I needed that I was alive. I was thankful that it was the middle of the night because that meant less traffic. If I could make it a little longer, I could find a hotel and get some sleep. It didn't even have to be fancy. A bed, a shower, and a toilet. That's all I required tonight.

There hadn't been many options as far as a place to lay my head for the night. Sure, I'd passed some cities, but I craved the blessed quietness of a small town. If I could just make it a little farther.

There! The sign creeping up on my right boasted the name of a town I'd never heard of before. Spiceland. I'd spotted the *Welcome to Indiana* sign some time ago and this was the first town I'd come across that seemed small enough for my purposes. It sounded like heaven. I hadn't passed much, other than fields, for the last forty miles or so. I slowed down to take the exit. I was fading fast, but I'd made it this far and forced myself to go just a little farther. The exit signs told me that I only had to go a few miles to get to the little no-tell motel. I turned right off the exit and kept going.

Every direction I looked I saw fields. Maybe this had been a mistake. There weren't even any other vehicles on this road. Everything was starting to get blurry. Shit! I wasn't going to make it. I felt the rumble strips under my tires, and despite the vibrations reminding me of the pain I was in, they still weren't enough to keep me awake. The blackness was closing in. There were no streetlights in this place, and I could no longer see where I was going. Trying to get my eyes to focus, I barely made out the sign for the motel. I'd been running on pure adrenaline and I had used up the last of my reserves.

That's the last thing I thought before my world went dark.

2

MICAH

"Micah!"

The pool cue slipped through my fingers and clumsily knocked the cue ball, causing me to miss my shot. "What the fuck, Aiden?"

I guess I'd zoned out a bit and wasn't taking my turn fast enough. I'd been doing that a lot lately. Getting lost in the maze of my thoughts. *Damn, I need to get laid.* There was a time I would have had no problem going out and making it happen. I still didn't have a problem making it happen…at least not the finding a woman part. I just don't get anything from it anymore. Sex used to be a good way to fight off my demons. Find a woman, fuck her senseless, become so sated and tired that I couldn't think, go home. Repeat. Repeat. Repeat. Problem was I didn't want those mindless fucks. They left me feeling…empty. I craved more. I needed more.

It was Saturday night and that meant that the Broken Rebel Brotherhood was out on the town, shooting pool and drinking some beer. There weren't many options for fun in this little Indiana town, but it sure as shit beat driving to Indianapolis and dealing with the city. That would suck the life out of every last one of us. Too many people, too much noise. So, we came to Dusty's.

We loved Dusty's. The moment you walked through the door, there was a sense of camaraderie that no other little dive bar provided. Kara, the bartender, always had a welcoming smile. She could tell when you needed a refill, and no one flipped her shit when she cut them off or took their keys. On Saturdays, the place was as packed as it gets. All twenty tables and ten booths were full. There were another fourteen stools at the bar. There used to be sixteen, but a year or so back, a fight had broken out between two farmers and Dusty had never replaced them. His way of punishing those responsible, I guess. A jukebox belted out whatever country song the last person picked and it didn't stop until the doors were locked after last call. Right now, Scotty McCreary was wishing he had "Five More Minutes". *I hear ya man.* There wasn't really a dance floor, but Dusty had left enough space between the tables that if anyone got a bug up their butt to dance, they could.

"Are you going to shoot or stand there daydreaming?" Aiden asked.

"Leave him alone," Nell chimed in. Nell was not a woman you wanted to fuck with. She might look all sweet and innocent, with her strawberry-blond hair and girl-next-door looks, but she was far from it. She and Brie were both badass women and both had been Seals. Nell was here. Brie was not. She'd made her excuses, like she always did, but I figured she was going to her boyfriend's place. None of us liked Zach much, but he was never around. Hell, I didn't even know him. He had never been to the club, so we had never actually met.

"Dude, if your head isn't in the game, fine. Let Griffin take over." Aiden's sharp tone pulled me from my musings.

"Fine." I tossed my pool cue to Griffin and sat down. I

watched as my family continued to have fun and laugh it up. It was so good to be with them all again. It felt like old times. Mostly.

Something was missing for me.

I was thirty-four years old and the President of the Broken Rebel Brotherhood motorcycle club. Brotherhood was a bit misleading because Nell and Brie were part of our crew, but it fit. We were all veterans and we were all a bit broken.

When we were discharged from the military, we scattered across the country to lick our wounds. But I'd tracked them down four years ago. We came together in Indiana and found a place to call home.

We pooled our money, which we had a lot of, and were able to purchase an old farmhouse and the two hundred acres surrounding it. Ideal for our purposes. We had spent so much time serving our country and securing the freedom of our fellow Americans, that it didn't quite sit well with any of us to no longer do *anything.*

That was how the Broken Rebel Brotherhood was born. When we came back together, we were all scarred. Sleep, at least the uninterrupted by nightmares kind, didn't exist. Tempers were quick to be sparked. Not one of us felt like we had a purpose. And then one night, we were at a bar, drowning our sorrows, and it happened. A woman was being hassled by a few drunks and it got out of hand. Griffin was the first to notice. He slowly got up off his bar stool and signaled to the rest of us to follow. We did. We knew not to question Griff when he had that look. Man, did he have that look. Griff delivered the first punch and after that, we all jumped into the fray. Nell and Brie, too. All we knew was that the woman was scared.

We left the bar that night feeling the adrenaline pumping through our veins, and when we got back to the house, we had a hard time coming down off that high. We'd stayed up talking for hours. About nothing and about everything. After that night, we had become the go-to crew when someone was in trouble. We specialized in abuse cases. We had a lot right here in our little town. More than most would think. Since we all had our bikes and loved them, a motorcycle club felt natural. We only had two conditions for being a member: one, be a veteran; two, have a burning desire to help those that can't help themselves.

So, that's how I became the president of a motorcycle club. We weren't your stereotypical motorcycle club. We didn't push drugs or guns or anything like that. Quite the opposite. We had a solid relationship with law enforcement. We were the ones they called when the law stood in their way. We didn't break the law, but we walked that fine line between right and wrong. We attended fundraisers, organized community events, and fought for what's right. We started as five. We were currently twenty strong and continued to grow. There were always veterans that needed a home, a support system, a reason to breathe. And that's what we were, what we did. Because let's face it. We weren't gonna get that shit anywhere else.

Griffin's laughter broke me from my memories. It seemed Saturday nights were the only time I heard that anymore. I returned my attention back to the pool game and realized that it was almost time for last call. I had switched to water about an hour ago because I knew I had to drive my bike home. Nell was the DD tonight and had driven the Jeep so the other guys could ride home with her. I decided it was time to go. I needed to feel the freedom my bike would provide. I slowly stood and walked to my family.

"I'm out." All eyes turned to me.

"What?" I knew they wanted me to stay, but they weren't going to be too far behind me.

"You going to the main house or your cabin?" Aiden asked.

"I'll be at the main house for a while." We all had rooms in the main house and we each had our own cabins on the property. Nothing too fancy. Just two-bedroom, two-bathroom cabins with a kitchen and living room. It was the perfect set up. We had the space to build more cabins as more permanent members joined, but we also had a space where we had the solidarity we sometimes craved.

I tossed a few bills on the table and walked out of the bar. It had cooled off a little, and I was glad for my cut. While it didn't provide the best barrier during Indiana winters, it offered a nice shield against the wind on these cool spring nights. I strode to my Triumph Rocket III and straddled the seat. As I gripped the handlebars, a feeling washed over me. I couldn't explain it, but I'd learned to trust these 'feelings' and something told me that my night was far from over.

Driving down Highway 3, that feeling never left me. It was like a swirling in my gut that I couldn't ignore. I slowly breathed in and out as I watched the fields fly by. Deep breathing was a technique we'd all learned to help us deal with the anxiety our PTSD caused. It helped, most of the time. I was about ten miles from the main house when I noticed it. There was something in the field to the left.

What the hell is that?

I slowed Rhiannon and pulled across the road to park. Yes, I named my bike Rhiannon, after the Celtic goddess of the moon and inspiration. That's what she was for me. My inspiration to keep going, keep breathing. Yes, my bike was female. Anything that can vibrate my balls and send that tingling feeling up my spine had to be female. I kept my eyes trained on the massive *thing* I was seeing. *Is that a car?* It looked like a car that had flipped over on its side. After parking, I broke out into a run, trying not to slip and slide in the mud, and when I got closer, I realized that's exactly what I was seeing.

I halted when I reached the vehicle and prayed that there was no one inside. Of course, that was pretty pointless. It's not like the car got here by itself. But I hoped that whoever had wrecked had somehow managed to walk away. Not fucking likely. I continued to creep closer to the car. The smell was so strong I had to pull my t-shirt up over my nose. Smoke was pouring out the engine, and that was a bad sign.

That's when I noticed it. Something red through the window. Hair. There was someone in there, and when I got right up to the window and realized it was a woman, I pulled out my cell phone. I'd never noticed before how much time it took to punch in that passcode, but those precious seconds were seconds that killed me to waste.

"Aw, you miss me already?" Aiden's voice came over the line. Normally, Aiden's sense of humor was a great thing. It could pull any of us out of a funk quicker than anything else. Not now, though. Now I wanted to reach through the phone and strangle him. I was seeing red and it wasn't just the hair through the window.

"I've got trouble," I barked into the phone.

"What kind of trouble?" That was Griffin. Aiden must have answered on speaker phone.

"There's a flipped car in the field with a woman inside. I need the Jeep. I'm going to get her out and no way can I put her on Rhiannon."

They no longer laughed at me when I called my bike by name. How could they? They all did the same.

"We'll be there in five." Nell this time.

"Call Doc. We'll take her to the main house, and he can

tell us if she needs a hospital." Doc was the newest member of the BRB and a former Army medic. He had the medical training we would need. At least I hoped he did. If he could operate on soldiers in the middle of bum-fuck Egypt with little to no supplies, he could surely help this woman.

I knew we should call an ambulance, but that's not how we did things. While it might not be the case in this instance, we usually dealt with domestic violence victims, and they rarely wanted to go to the hospital. It was best to wait and get answers first. If Doc assessed her and said she needed a hospital, then she'd get one. But not yet.

"I'll call Doc and be sure he can meet us." That was Aiden.

Blood oozed down the side of the woman's face, contrasting greatly with an otherwise pale complexion. She would need some sort of medical attention.

While I waited for everyone, I tried to open the driver's side door. There was no movement in the car, and I wasn't sure if I was going to be bringing Doc a patient or a corpse. God, I hoped Doc would get the opportunity to work his magic. In order to get the door open, I had to climb up on to the side of the car. Fortunately, the woman had her seat belt on and while her unconscious body was dangling from the seat, she hadn't completely fallen to the side the car was resting on where gravity surely would have taken her. When the door gave way, I snaked my right arm in and grabbed her left. Something in me clicked. All my training came to the forefront of my brain and I began to do whatever was necessary to get her free.

I carried her about ten feet away from the car to lay her on the ground. Carrying dead weight, no pun intended, I hoped, was never easy, but I wasn't letting her go, no matter what. I couldn't see any of her features because it was so dark, but I could make out the blood. It was a sticky coating on her face, arms, and clothes. The smell of copper wafted

BROKEN SOULS

off of her. My PTSD chose that moment to try to sneak in, but I fought it. Breathe…in, out, in out. PTSD is a fickle bitch, but I was not bending to her will this time.

The squealing of tires sounded behind me, and I knew the cavalry had arrived. I heard the sound of the others running toward me as I checked for a pulse. It was there, but barely. Score one for Doc working some magic. As the other's got closer, I thought I heard something from the woman's lips.

"No…mmm…I can't…don't do this…no." Her voice was faint, barely above a whisper, but in that moment, I knew we wouldn't be calling the cops…officially. I would put a call in to Jackson, the Sheriff, because he was a friend and I knew he'd keep everything off the record. But that would have to come later. Once I knew exactly what we were dealing with. The beam of the flashlight Nell carried, likely out of the go-bag we kept stashed in the Jeep, caught my eye. I was finally able to take a good look at the woman's face and when I did, my heart went into a free fall.

"Fuck me," Nell whispered. "That's not all from a car accident. Some of those are old bruises."

"Looks that way," I replied. I wish I could say the sight of old bruising shocked me, but with what we did, not much surprised me at that point. There was a three-inch gash on the woman's right temple that clearly needed stitches. Her shirt was torn and had risen up her belly while I had carried her and I could see the angry bruises beginning to form on her sides, along her ribs, and disappearing beneath her baggy sweatpants. There were other bruises on both arms, of varying colors and phases of healing, in the shape of handprints. There were some scars marring her flesh. She was wearing those little white shoes, Keds I think they're called, with no socks. I could see the scars on her ankles indicating to me that her feet had been tied up at some point. There wasn't an inch of her dingy clothing that wasn't caked in blood. It wasn't completely dry, but I still wondered how long she'd been here. Alone. Bleeding. *Dying.*

"Help me get her to the Jeep. Nell, you can follow on Rhiannon. Someone call Brie. I don't give a fuck if she doesn't want to leave Zach right now. Get her home. We need all the hands we can get. Move!" I was in the zone. That zone where I was still the commanding officer of our team and could hand out orders.

The rest happened so fast. Griffin helped me carry her to the car and we gently laid her in the back seat. I drove because I was the most sober. Aiden was beside me. Griffin sat in the backseat with the woman's head in his lap. When I started the Jeep, a moan came from the back of the car. My eyes snapped to Griffin's in the rear-view mirror.

"Just drive. She's not waking up and the sooner we get her to Doc, the better." That's Griffin for you. So matter of fact, but exactly right. The laughter from earlier was gone and the Griffin of the last four years was back.

As I drove to the house, my mind raced with all the questions that were routine in our line of work. Where had she come from? What was her name? Who, or what, had done this to her? These were questions that I knew I wouldn't be getting answers to anytime soon, but I wanted to ask them all the same.

I pulled into the driveway a few minutes later and parked right next to the porch, not caring if I tore up the yard. It wouldn't be hard to do with the soaking rain we'd had for the past two days. The porch was wide and wrapped around the front of the farmhouse. The house was built in the 1800s and had needed a lot of work when we bought it. But we put in the work and now it was beautiful. I didn't see any of it at the moment, however. Nell pulled in right beside us and cut off Rhiannon. I noticed Doc's bike in the driveway, so I knew he was here.

Doc chose that moment to come barreling out of the front door. The screen door slammed into the side of the house and screeched as it swung closed. Doc was down the steps and peering into the car as I opened the back door. It took some maneuvering, but we managed to get the woman out of the Jeep and into the house.

"Take her to my room." I had the only room on the first floor and had never been as glad for that as I was right then. It was a logical decision to take the room downstairs. I was the president. I was the first line of defense should any of our good deeds bring trouble to our door. Now it just made things easier.

Griffin and I laid Red down on the bed. That's what I had begun to think of her as. Red. That was the only feature I had been able to make out in the darkness and now, as the light touched it, her hair looked like fire. The most glorious fire I had ever seen. The kind of fire you sat around on a summer night with your buddies, enjoying the easier side of life. I could also see the blood more clearly, but between the streaks on her face, I noticed porcelain skin with a bit of freckles. As she had yet to wake up, I couldn't see her eyes. But I bet they were green. Don't redheads usually have green eyes?

While I waited for Doc to grab his supplies, I pulled out my cell and snapped some pictures of Red. I didn't want to take a chance that none of this was documented. You never knew when evidence would be needed. I saved the photos to my phone and shot off a quick text to Jackson.

Me: Come when you can. Have a new case.

I knew Jackson trusted us to do what was necessary and he would get here when he got here. For now, that part of the job was done.

Doc arrived with his black medical bag and he and Nell carried bowls of water, towels and whatever else they could fit in their arms. He began to clean up Red, barking orders at Nell, as she was his right-hand woman during medical emergencies. My eyes raked over Red's body and took in as much as I could. The more blood that was washed away, the more I felt like I had seen Red before. But where?

3

SADIE

I moaned when something freezing hit my burning skin. *What the hell was happening? Was I being dunked in ice?* Wanting to escape the sensation, I allowed myself to be sucked back into my dreams.

"Sadie, I'd like you to meet Ms. Camden. You're going to be staying with her for a while," the social worker said. I wanted to go home but I knew that couldn't happen. I didn't have a home or parents to go back to. At 6 years old, this was my third foster home. I knew that I would likely not be here long. I was never in one place long.

"Sadie, it's nice to meet you," Ms. Camden sounded pleasant, but so did the people at the last house I was dropped off at.

I tossed and turned as the images in my head shifted. I could hear a distant voice and I wanted to reach out and latch onto it, but I couldn't.

"Sadie, I'd like you to meet Mr. and Mrs. Mallory. You're going to be staying with them for a while." The social worker appeared bored as she introduced me to the eighth couple I would be living with. I knew the routine. Meet the family. Learn their rules. Get

comfortable. Move. This had been my routine for the last thirteen years.

"Hi Sadie. It's wonderful to meet you. Please, call us Sylvia and Clay. We're so happy that you're here," Mrs. Mallory said.

"Hey," I said, looking at the floor. "Where's my room?"

"We'll show you around in a few minutes, if that's okay with you. Let's get the necessary paperwork out of the way with Miss Shell first," Mr. Mallory said. His voice was deep but quiet. I liked that.

"She's having another nightmare. Can't you do something for her?"

I didn't know who that was, but it wasn't Mr. or Mrs. Mallory. They were quiet and calm. This voice was gravelly. Sexy. *Am I dead?* Because heaven was the only place I'd be hearing a voice that sex-inspiring.

"What the fuck do you think I can give her for a nightmare? With the nightmares that you've had, has a doctor ever given you something for it? No!"

Huh. I didn't know that voice either, but he sounded pissed. That couldn't be good.

"Fine. I'll be back."

I heard footsteps and then the quiet click of a door shutting. That had been sexy voice. *Come back!*

My dream turned into a nightmare as I fell back to the first time Ian hit me.

Wringing my hands, I waited for Ian to get home from work. He liked me to have dinner on the table when he walked through the door and I'd managed to always make it happen. Until tonight. I heard the door from the garage to the kitchen open and jumped up from my seat at the table.

"Hi, honey," I said, trying to inject some cheer into my voice.

"Where's dinner?" he said as he looked at the empty table.

The power had gone out earlier in the day and had yet to come back on. I couldn't cook. I had briefly thought about going into town to get some takeout but that was before I remembered that I no longer had a working car. I hated to disappoint him because that always ended with him yelling at me or worse, giving me the silent treatment.

"Well—"

"Fuck, Sadie!" he interrupted. "I work hard all damn day so you can have all of this," sweeping his hand to encompass the house he continues, "and all I ask is that you have dinner ready when I get home. You can't even do that right."

"Ian, the power went out and I couldn't—"

"Shut up! I don't want to hear your excuses. You're an ungrateful bitch, you know that?" Ian was pacing as he yelled and something was different this time. He seemed agitated. Sure, he'd called me names before but this seemed like...more. Normally, I would've taken his shit, but not this time. Not when he was being unreasonable about something entirely out of my control.

"Ungrateful? I don't think so. I do everything around here while you go to a cushy job and rake in the money. Money that I never see a dime of. No, I do everything you want, no questions asked and this is how you treat me? Not happening." I stood right in front of him, my chest heaving. That's when I realized my mistake. Ian backhanded me across the face. Too stunned to speak, I turned on my heel, ran to the bedroom and slammed the door. I could hear Ian stomping down the hallway to follow me and I knew I was powerless to stop him from coming in if he wanted to.

"No!" Jolting upright on the bed, pain radiated through my body. I looked around to find the room empty and began to relax. That didn't last long because the door was thrown open and a behemoth of a man came running in.

"Are you okay?" I recognized that voice from earlier. The one that was...sexy.

"Who are you?" I asked.

Relief crossed the man's features a split second before he spoke. "My name is Micah."

Another man, not quite as large but just as intimidating, came through the doorway.

"What happened?" the new man asked.

"She yelled, so I came in to see if she was okay," Sexy Voice said.

"Are you hurting, honey? Do you need more pain meds?" New Man asked, as he poked and prodded at my injuries. I knew I should probably ask his name. I couldn't find my voice, so I shrugged instead and winced as he touched me. "I'll bet you're hurting a lot, but I'll take care of that." He reached in a black bag that was sitting next to the bed and pulled out a syringe. He walked toward me, and that's when I saw the IV sticking out of the back of my hand.

"What the hell's in there?" I angled my head toward the IV bag. I may have been in pain, but I'd be damned if I'd sit still and let myself be drugged. I didn't know who these people were or what they had planned for me. I wanted to get up and leave, but I didn't have the strength.

"It's something for the pain," New Man said as he pushed the plunger on the syringe and injected the liquid into the IV. "You should start feeling better in a few minutes."

"I don't need anything for pain," I lied, trying to stop whatever was about to be shot into my bloodstream.

"Sweetness, you need to let Doc do his thing," Sexy Voice pleaded. "I can see blood dripping from some of your stitches so Doc's going to check those out once the meds kick in." His lips kept moving but the words started to sound far away.

"What did you give me?" I demanded one more time. Doc dug in his bag and brought out what looked like black thread and needles. My vision started to blur, so I couldn't be sure. I tried to fight the feeling of being sucked under, but eventually, I lost and my nightmares returned.

Micah

I had to get away. I couldn't watch as Red thrashed on the bed while Doc did his thing. I knew that Doc did what he had to, but that hadn't made it any easier. The moans that had escaped Red's lips shot straight through me. And what lips they were. Plump and kissable. I bet they'd feel like wet, hot velvet wrapped around my cock. Not the right time, but I couldn't seem to help it. Those moans were not something out of a fantasy, as they were triggered from pain, but my dick hadn't seemed to care. So, yeah, I left the room.

"You okay?"

I whipped my head around. Griffin was leaning back against the wall with his arms crossed over his chest. A storm brewed in his eyes, but he remained calm. That's why he was my vice president. He had the strength, stamina, intensity, and passion to do what needed to be done while always remaining calm. It seemed like nothing ever got to him. He was loyal, almost to a fault, and he was my best friend.

"No. No, I'm not okay. You saw her. That's not all from the roll over."

"I don't think so either. But, man, you have to get a grip. We see this kind of thing all the time. We protect people from this every damn day. If you start letting it get to you like this, you can't do what needs doing."

I knew he was right. Being a Seal, we'd seen the shadiest parts of human nature that you could imagine. And then there's what we did with BRB. In a small town, the majority of what we handled were abuse situations and it took a toll on each of us in completely different ways. I would never change what we did. I could never regret helping the people we saved. But sometimes I struggled to understand the *why* of it all.

"You're right. I know you're right. I just needed a minute. Thanks man, I'm okay now."

The look that crossed Griffin's face told me he hadn't bought it, but he let it go. It was time to change the subject. "Where the hell is Brie? She should be here by now."

"I just got a text from her." Something flashed in his eyes as he spoke, but I was too caught up in my own head to even try to dissect what it was. "She should be here any minute."

Griffin turned to walk away, but I stopped him.

"When she gets here, send her to me."

"Go easy on her Mic. Something's going on with her and I'm not sure it's all related to Zach. I know you want her here, and yes, she should be here, but we don't own her. The BRB doesn't own her."

I nodded once at Griffin before he was gone. I pushed myself away from the wall and went back through the heavy door to my room. My eyes zeroed in on my bed and Red. Doc had her clean and had pulled the sheet up over her body in an attempt to preserve some modesty. Having noticed her bloody clothes in a pile by my dresser, I knew she was naked under that sheet. Doc was gingerly putting stitches in the gash on her temple. Protectiveness surged through me at the sight.

I walked over to the bed. Kneeling next to it, I picked up her delicate hand in my much larger one. As Doc worked, Red moaned and her head thrashed from side to side.

"Shh. Calm down sweetness. Shh. You're okay," I crooned. Amazingly enough, she stilled. It wasn't lost on me that I was talking to her much like I would a friend or a lover. I remained at her side until Doc was done repairing the damage to the stitches on her face. She remained calm through it all. I whispered to her the whole time. I have no idea what I said. I just kept talking. Anything to keep her calm.

As Doc slowly started to pull the sheet down Red's body, Brie came through the door. Someone must have given her a head's up because she was stealthily quiet. As she took in the scene before her, her eyes grew almost comically round. I didn't know if the look was for me or for the woman in the bed. We'd helped a lot of women over the years and I'd never allowed myself to get this close. Make it this personal.

"Jesus, Micah. What happened?" Brie asked. I knew how hard it was for Brie to show restraint. She was normally very quick to act. Some would call her a ballbuster, a badass. I would agree, but you'd never hear me call her that out loud. I liked my family jewels too much.

I quietly filled Brie in on what had happened. As I spoke, a sheen of tears filled Brie's eyes and a few spilled over and down her cheeks. I made a mental note to ask her about that later because Brie didn't cry. I'd seen her stare down an enemy without so much as flinching. I'd seen her in hand-to-hand combat in the bowels of hell. I'd seen her hold a fellow soldier as they drew their last breath. I'd been to countless funerals with her. The funerals of our fallen brothers and sisters, and she hadn't shed a tear.

"What do you want me to do?" Brie asked. Back in control. That was the Brie I knew.

"I need you to go outside with Griff, Aiden and Nell and do some recon around the house. For obvious reasons, I don't have all the facts, but this shit doesn't feel right. I don't recall anyone following us to the house, but I can't be sure. Make sure the property is secure and then I want someone standing guard at every entrance at all times. Go wake up the newbies if you have to. Get them to help. Everyone can take shifts. I don't care how it happens, so long as it does."

Brie nodded and started back for the door. She was a stark contrast to the woman in my bed. Brie really was a beautiful woman, but not for me. Not only was she not my type, but I would never cross that line. She was like a sister to me, and I was worried about her. I added it to my list of growing concerns.

"Wait," I called out to Brie before she crossed the threshold. "Do you trust Zach?"

"Where are you going with this, Micah? Don't you have bigger things to worry about right now than my relationship?" She sounded resigned as she asked this and tilted her head towards the woman in my bed.

"I do and this isn't about your relationship. We'll discuss that...later. I'm asking because I know he does some towing on the side, and her car is still in that field. Until we know exactly what's going on, I need someone we can trust to tow it. Do you trust him to do that? Can he keep his mouth shut?" I was angry at having to explain myself, but that wasn't Brie's fault and I had to keep that in mind.

"Yeah, I can ask him to do that, but I'm not sure he will." The look on her face was full of apology, like she knew her response would piss me off. "It would help if we could throw a little cash his way since he can't really bill anyone for it. I'll throw him fifty bucks."

"The fuck you will! He can send an invoice to the club and we'll pay it like any other customer. If he has a problem with that, tell him to call me."

"Okay, Micah."

Brie spent the next few minutes texting Zach. Her back was to me through it all and tension coiled my muscles every time a frustrated sigh came from her direction. When she turned back to me, she looked angry, and a bit sad.

"He can't tow the car, but has a guy who can." She kept her gaze level with mine, never wavering. "What do you want me to tell him?"

"Forget it. I'll have one of the guys get out there to tow it."

I pulled out my cell and started to send off texts to make that happen.

Brie didn't speak before she turned and started towards the door.

"Brie?" I lifted my eyes from my phone and my voice stopped her in her tracks.

She glanced over her shoulder. "Yeah?"

"Thanks, I appreciate you trying." Brie left the room.

I turned my attention back to the text I'd been typing and breathed a sigh of relief that one of the newer recruits was free to tow the car. That crisis averted, I glanced at Red. Her eyes remained closed and free of blood but they shifted back and forth under the lids. I was sure she was having a nightmare. It didn't take a genius to figure out that her road to that field had been paved by a shitstorm.

4

MICAH

"Why didn't you call this in?" Jackson asked me, looking a little put out.

"I texted you." He was acting like it was my fault he'd taken four days to get here. "Besides, we don't know what happened to her beyond that car accident. You saw her. You saw the pictures. No way are all her injuries from the night I found her!" I slammed my hand down on my desk. We were talking in the library so we had a little privacy, but that sound would carry beyond the door.

"Yeah, I know, but still. I have to make an effort of protesting your actions. I am the sheriff after all," Jackson chuckled as he said this. I knew he was trying to make me feel better, but it didn't work.

"Jackson, I'm not saying that the law can't get involved. Fuck, I know they have to. I'm asking you to give me a week, maybe two, to try to get some answers. If there's someone after her, and my gut tells me that if there isn't right now, there will be soon, then we need to protect her. I just want to see what we're up against first. Can you give me that time?

Please?" I felt like I was begging, but this meant more to me than our usual cases.

"I'll give you two weeks. I'd say one, but it may take her that long to feel comfortable talking and I don't want to have to hear you beg again. Jesus." Jackson sighed and ran his fingers through his hair. "I need you to understand something though, Micah. This case is no different than any other we've worked together on, at least not as far as I'm concerned. You need to always at least make an effort to keep everything above board. I will give you the time you're requesting, as a courtesy, because I know the BRB does good work and we rely on you for a lot. I also know you'll protect her. But if at the end of that two weeks you don't have some answers, I will do what is necessary to get some myself. And I expect regular updates over the next two weeks. This is my town, and I don't want there to be any surprises. Are we clear?"

"Yeah, we're clear. Thanks, Jackson."

After Jackson left, I hopped on Rhiannon. After four days of not leaving Red, other than to use the bathroom, I was starting to stink. I could shower at the main house, but Nell and Brie had assured me they would sit with Red while I went to my cabin. I was worried about leaving her, but Doc assured me she needed the rest for her body to heal and it was okay if I left for a bit.

The ride to my cabin helped to rejuvenate me. Or at least it gave me the feeling of being refreshed. When I parked in my driveway, I hopped off my bike and jogged up the three steps to my front porch. I strode through the door, and instantly, I was home. Not just the physical actuality of being home, but the feeling that I got when I was there. Sure, having a *place* helped, but it was the feeling, the emotion, the people that made a place a home. I had learned that the hard way.

When I was fifteen, my parents died in a car accident. They had been out celebrating their anniversary when a drunk driver hit them head-on. I remembered the cops showing up at our door and asking if I had any other family with me or if there was someone I could call. I had seen a lot of cop shows and it was never good when they showed up at your door. Besides being an insolent teenager, I was scared, so I flipped them shit. After going a verbal round, I gave them the number to my Gram and Pap, and ever since that night, I'd lived with my grandparents. Better than in foster care, I guess. I knew I wasn't the easiest to deal with, but deal with me they did.

When I was a senior in high school, I began to hang around the wrong crowd. I got arrested one night for underage drinking, and when my Pap had picked me up at the station I could see the anger seething off him. But he'd shocked me. He hadn't yelled. He'd just calmly signed the paperwork so I could go home with him and assured the police officer that I would be dealt with. When we got home, he and Gram sat me down and gave me two choices. I could either continue down the path I was on, and if I got arrested again, I wouldn't be welcome in their home. *Or*, I could enlist in the military and always have a home to go back to. It hadn't taken me long to decide. I wanted a home.

When I graduated high school, I immediately went to the nearest military recruiting office and joined up. Best thing I'd ever done. Not only would I always have a home, but I had gained a new family. I put in my time and eventually worked my way into the Navy Seals. I was that damn good. Hell, I was still that damn good. Then *it* happened. The mission that forever changed the course of my career and my life.

Thoughts of that mission usually kick-started my PTSD, so I pushed them away.

As I walked through the bedroom to the bathroom, I

bumped into the overstuffed chair that Brie and Nell had picked when they 'helped' me decorate. I didn't care about the look of the place much, as long as it wasn't too girly, which it wasn't, so I let them pick the color scheme and furniture. The only thing I had required was a top of the line kitchen, no expense spared, with granite countertops and stainless-steel appliances. Nell had mercilessly teased me about it, because I didn't like to cook, unless it was on a grill, and she'd accused me of doing it with a woman in mind. Well, no shit! Of course, I had. Someday I hoped to be married with a few kids, and I liked living here with the others, so I wanted my future wife to be comfortable here. I didn't tell them that, though. Wasn't giving them the satisfaction.

As I stepped into the shower and let the water wash away the last few days of my vigil, an image of Red popped into my head. Not the woman lying in my bed in the main house but the beauty of my fantasies. The woman that wasn't battered and bruised. The woman that had a body made for sin. *Fuck*. I felt like a randy teenager who only needed a mental image to come. And quickly at that.

As the warm water continued to cascade down my back, I took my cock in my hand and gave it a good squeeze. No use wasting a perfectly good boner. My images of Red shifted from the wounded woman I rescued to a goddess in my bed. Still the same Red, but naked and begging for my cock to pound into her pussy. Pump, pump, pump, squeeze. In my fantasy, her wet folds encased my dick like a glove. She was hot and I was close. Pump, pump, pump. I blew my load and it covered the shower wall. Jesus, I needed to get laid. Unfortunately for my dick, I didn't want to get laid by just anyone.

I rinsed off the aftermath and finished my shower. It was time to get back to her. I'd wasted enough time and the proverbial clock was ticking with the deadline Jackson had given me. I quickly got dressed and grabbed extra clothes so that I could stay up at the main house for a few more days without leaving. Walking outside, I pulled the door shut behind me, hopped off the porch steps and got back on Rhiannon. Five more minutes and I'd see her again and hopefully get some answers.

5

SADIE

My head felt like it was going to explode. I wanted to open my eyes, but I was afraid. Had Ian found me? I could hear what sounded like snoring, but I wasn't sure. Ian didn't snore, so I was confused. I opened my eyes a fraction, immediately slamming them closed as the light blinded me. I lay there for a few more minutes, mentally trying to get my bearings and came up empty.

Where am I? What happened? And for the love of all that's holy, who the fuck is snoring? I wiggled my fingers and toes and tried to move. My mouth was so dry, and as I ran my tongue over my teeth, I felt a fuzzy coating. *Ew.* I lay still for a minute and that was when I noticed the snoring had stopped.

My eyes snapped open and right above me was a man. I scrambled up to my knees, ignored the mind-numbing pain, tried to scoot back on the bed, and threw my arms up in front of my face.

"Whoa. Hey now, sweetness. It's okay. I'm not going to hurt you." That voice. I knew that voice. It was the voice from heaven. He held his hands up in a gesture of surrender.

He sounded nice enough, but I couldn't be sure. I remembered the soothing words he'd said before, but I was still on high alert.

"Where am I? Who the fuck are you?" Oh my God, was that my voice? I sounded like a frog croaking.

"I'm Micah. You don't remember me telling you that a few days ago?"

"No, I don't. I have to go. I have to get out of here before Ian comes back!" I was panicking, but I didn't care. I just had to go.

"Ian? Who's Ian?"

"What do you mean, who's Ian? You work for him, don't you?"

"No, sweetness. I don't work for Ian. I have no idea what you're talking about. And you're in my clubs' home. In my room." I slowly lowered my hands and looked at the stranger standing next to the bed.

He sounded sincere, and even though I was scared, I forced myself to hold onto the fact that he'd done nothing but try to help me. *Maybe I am safe with him.*

"Sweetness, you need to try to relax. I'm going to go get Doc to come check out your wounds and see if you've torn any of your stitches again. He can give you some more pain meds if you need them." As Sexy Voice…no wait, he said his name was Micah. As Micah turned to cross the room and fetch this 'Doc' guy, I took a moment and assessed him. He was big, no doubt about it. And for a moment, I wondered if he was big all over. Wasn't the right time, but damn! He was so tall, easily six foot three, a foot taller than me. His hair was jet black and a little too long, but somehow, it worked. Tattoos peeked out from beneath the sleeves of his white t-shirt and he was wearing a black leather vest with patches on it. I hadn't gotten a good look at his face, and I eagerly waited for him to turn around so I could. Muscles bunched under his leather vest and I wondered what they would feel like under my hands. And that ass. He sure could fill out a pair of jeans. Disappointment flooded my system when he turned back around to face me.

"My eyes are up here, sweetness." There was a hint of a smile in that statement and I raised my eyes and looked into his. Wow. The grayest eyes I'd ever seen stared back at me. They were a light gray that reminded me of a summer sky after it had rained. There were creases at the corners of his eyes and I wondered if they were from laughter or worry. His face had some stubble on it, like he hadn't shaved in a few days. He looked like sin…and just a little scary.

Micah frowned and then a huge grin bloomed across his face, at about the same speed my panties got wet.

"Blue. Huh."

"What?" I croaked. His stare was so intense, I could feel the panic well up inside of me again.

"Your eyes. They're *blue.* I would have bet my last dollar they would be green. But they're blue. They remind me of forget-me-nots."

Micah's stare became more intense before he said, "Oh my God, I know who you are."

~

Micah

I knew the moment the words were out of my mouth I had fucked up, but the filter between my brain and my mouth had quit working when it hit me how I knew her. The look of fear in Red's eyes was something I would never forget.

"Shit. I know how that sounded."

"What do you mean, you know me? I thought you said

you didn't know Ian." Leave it to a woman to miss the part where I compared her eyes to a beautiful flower.

"Forget I said that. Can you answer a few questions for me?"

"Forget you…no, I most certainly cannot forget you just said that. What did you mean?"

"It's going to sound crazy but…"

"Just spit it out, dammit!"

I could tell if I didn't just 'spit it out', as she so aptly put it, the hole I had started to dig was going to get deeper.

"Is your name Sadie?" I nervously waited for her response.

"How do you know that?"

"So, you are her? I thought so." I could tell that I wasn't making any sense to Sadie, but I was still trying to process it myself. I'd never actually met her, but I'd seen her at a distance. I remembered my Gram talking about the foster child she and Pap had taken in. I was in the military by then and had never made it home to meet her in person. Then Pap had died. I was able to get emergency leave to go home for the funeral and Sadie had been there. I had seen her standing by the casket, staring down at Pap's lifeless body. As I was hugging Gram, Sadie had turned around and we had locked eyes. After a split second, she had turned and ran. She locked herself in the bathroom and refused to come out. Gram and I had left to give her some space, but when we went back to check on her, she was gone. After the funeral was over, Gram and I had tried to find her for a few days before I had to return for duty, but we failed.

As I reined in my thoughts, I gazed back at the frightened woman in my bed. She was still huddled in the corner, as if she was afraid I was going to hurt her. I tried to let the tension ease from my body so I wouldn't look so threatening, but it was hard. I wanted to call Gram and tell her I'd found her. I wanted to ask Sadie why she had left. I needed answers. I knew grilling her wasn't the key to unlocking this mystery. At least not right now. Phone call first, questions later.

"I'll be right back," I said to Sadie. Then I turned on my heel, walked out of the room and closed the door behind me. I pulled out my phone and called Gram.

"Hello," Gram's voice came over the line.

"Hi Gram."

"Oh, honey, it's so good to hear from you! It's been too long since you've called."

Guilt slammed into me. She was right. It *had* been too long since I'd called her. "I'm sorry, we've been busy. We had a case that had us running ragged for a while." The BRB didn't hide what we did. Our families, the community, they all knew what we did and what we stood for. And thank God they supported us.

"I'm sorry to hear that. I hope everything worked out."

"Yeah. Yeah it did. It was a close call though. In the end we were able to get the mother and her two young children to another state. Taught that bastard of an ex-husband a lesson while we were at it."

"Language! Anyway, I'm glad to hear it. We need more people like you and your little group in the world." I snorted as she said that. She didn't always understand, but she always respected. Supported.

"Gram, I actually called for a reason. I wanted to tell you about our latest case."

"Micah, you never give me details. If you want to tell me, I'll listen, but why now?"

"Because I'm fairly certain you know this one." I heard her indrawn breath and I wished I didn't have to do this over the phone.

"How could I know her? It is a her, right?" she asked.

"Yes, Gram, she's a woman. Are you sitting down because I think this is going to come as a big shock to you?"

"Just tell me, Micah," she pleaded, "I can handle it."

"I'm almost positive it's Sadie."

Silence.

"Sadie? My Sadie?" she finally asked. "How can that be? What is she doing there?"

"Gram, I don't have a lot of answers yet," I explained. "Can you do me a favor? I need to know for sure it's her. I took a picture shortly after finding her and I want to send it to you to see if you recognize her. Would that be okay?"

"Of course, it's okay. I can't believe Sadie's there! Oh, my heavens, Micah, I want to see her." I could hear her sobbing, and I wished I could be with her.

"In time, Gram. For now, I need you to look at the picture. But Gram," I paused, "I need to warn you the picture is not pretty. She was in pretty rough shape when I found her. I hate to ask you to look at it, but I need to know for sure if it's her."

"Micah Jacob Mallory, I am not some frail old woman that can't handle a little blood," she scolded. I didn't correct her because she is eighty-seven and it's more than a little blood.

"Sorry, Gram. I just want you to be prepared. I'll send the picture through text as soon as we hang up."

"Okay honey."

"Thanks, Gram. I gotta go. I'll call you in a few days. Maybe in the next few weeks I can bring Sadie to Pennsylvania to see you."

"Oh, that would be wonderful honey. And Micah? Go do something fun. You sound worn out and stressed. I worry about you. It took you so long to get past the worst of the PTSD and I would hate to see you spiral again. I love you."

"I love you too, Gram. Watch for that text," I reminded her, "Talk to you later."

I sent her the text as soon as I ended the call and her response confirmed my suspicions.

Gram: Yes, that's Sadie. She looks horrible. What happened to her?

Me: I don't know everything yet, but I'll keep you posted.

Gram: You better! Take care of my girl.

Me: I will. I promise.

6

SADIE

As I watched Micah leave and then gently close the door, my thoughts began to riot. How did he know my name? What did he mean, he knew who I was? I had to get out of there. I needed to find my car and get driving. Shit! My car. As I thought that, the accident came slamming back into my memory like a runaway freight train. The memories scared me, but I had to keep moving. I refused to be a victim. I had spent so much time planning my escape and I wasn't going to fuck it up by freaking out.

I started to scoot across the bed and when I reached the edge, I pulled my legs out from under my ass, kicked them forward and planted my feet on the floor. So far, so good. Every inch of me hurt, but I could do this. I pushed myself up with my hands. I swayed and back down on my ass I went. I tried again and then again. It took me five times trying to stand before I didn't fall right back down. Once I was up, it hit me. *I was naked!* I needed clothes. I noticed some blood seeping from where I had pulled my stitches when I panicked, but I ignored it. I could clean up later.

I gingerly stepped toward the dresser on the opposite

wall. I opened the top drawer and all I saw were boxers and socks. I tugged open the next drawer and that was just t-shirts and jeans. I grabbed a black t-shirt and clutched it in my hand. I wouldn't even try to get dressed until I had everything. I knew it would tire me out and I needed to be smart about this. I tugged on the third drawer and hit pay dirt. Sweatpants. It wasn't likely that any of Micah's pants would fit me, but if I could find a pair with a drawstring, it was better than nothing. Nothing sucked. I pulled out a pair of gray sweats and I was in luck. I saw the white drawstring hanging on the inside of the pants at the waistband.

I held the shirt and pants in my hand like my life depended on them. As I made my way back to the bed, I heard the squeak of the door opening. I froze. The clothes fell to the floor. I couldn't move. My eyes burned and tears threatened to spill, but I didn't care. I had been so close!

"Get out!" As soon as the sound of Micah's voice hit my ears, I jumped. The next thing I knew there was a soft blanket being draped over my shoulders and Micah circled in front of me. I lowered my head to hide my fear, my tears, my nakedness. God, I was a hot mess.

"Look at me, sweetness." He placed his knuckles under my chin and tried to tip it up. I tried to resist, but it was pointless. I had no strength left. I looked at him and what I saw floored me. There was a tenderness in his eyes that I'd never seen before. Well, not never, but not in a long fucking time. That tenderness scared me because I couldn't trust it. I made that mistake once and I'd be damned if I did it again. I tried to pull away, but Micah was having none of it.

"I'm sorry I yelled. Doc was right behind me and when I saw you standing there naked, all I could think was that I didn't want him to see. Crazy, right? He's seen you naked for the past week while he tended your wounds."

"Wait. What? Did you say week? I've been here for a week?"

"Yes. You've been in and out of consciousness for a week straight. Thank God for Doc and his magic." There was that smile in his voice again. "For the first few days you fought us pretty hard, but you finally just settled into a deep sleep. You had a fever for a while and everyone wanted to call an ambulance, but I wouldn't let them. Something told me not to. I hope I made the right decision."

"Um, yes, I guess. And you said everyone. Who is everyone? And I'll ask you again, where the hell am I?"

"Right to the point. I like your sass. Despite the hell you have so obviously been through, you still manage to cut straight through the bullshit. And everyone is Doc, Aiden, Nell, Griffin, and Brie. There are others, but those are the ones that are here the most."

He had said he liked my sass. I didn't have sass. Well, I hadn't had sass in a long time. Crap. While I didn't want to be a victim, I didn't want to upset him either. I was so tired and based on the debacle of trying to get dressed, I didn't think I could manage to escape just yet. I needed to keep Micah happy so he'd let me stay and I sure as hell didn't want to piss him off. Ian's beatings had been bad enough. I could only imagine the pain Micah could inflict on me in anger. Falling back on old habits, I loosened my grip on the blanket and it started to fall from my shoulders.

"Jesus. What are you doing?" Micah rasped as he lunged to grab the blanket and wrapped it around me.

I shifted from foot to foot and fidgeted with my hands. I knew I must look bad. But if what Micah had said was true, and I had been out for a week, some of the bruises had to be starting to fade. I couldn't look as bad as I did on day one. I wasn't model material or anything, but I had curves and a pretty nice set of tits and I hoped that Micah was a titman so he'd let me stay. I needed Micah to get on board with this plan, so I could crawl back in the bed. I was fading fast.

"I'm sorry. I just…"

"Just what, Sadie?" He sounded angry and I could see a ticking in his jaw.

"I didn't mean to upset you and I know you probably want me to go and I don't want to bother you or put any of you or your friends out and I know this is your bed and you must be tired and I don't want you to be mad and I didn't mean to sass you and I thought if I could make you happy and you liked what you saw we could work out a trade because I'm really tired and I just want to lie down for a little while and then—"

Micah threw his hands up in the air, effectively cutting off my tirade. Probably a good thing because I had been running out of air and felt a little woozy and lightheaded. So much for not being a victim.

Micah scooped me up in his arms, carried me to the bed and gently placed me on the mattress. I could still see the ticking in his jaw. He sat down beside me on the edge of the bed and sighed.

"First of all, do not apologize for your sass. I love it. Second, don't ever apologize for speaking your mind or standing up for yourself or for demanding answers. Third, I hope to God that you weren't suggesting that you have to pay me for my kindness with sexual favors. I don't work like that. I'm not going to lie and say that I don't like a good fuck, because I do. I am a man after all. But I have never forced a woman to do something she doesn't want to do and I sure as shit ain't starting now. I can tell that you haven't had good experiences where the male species are concerned, but sweetness, I'm going to show you that not all men are snakes." Micah breathed in deeply through his nose and then released it through his mouth.

"I'm sor—"

"If you say you're sorry one more time, we're going to have issues, you and me. The last thing I want to tell you before I get Doc back in here to check your wounds, is this. You are welcome here in the main house for as long as you need to be here. Shit, you're welcome anywhere on this property. You will be protected, and no one will hurt you. The BRB will do whatever is necessary to ensure that. Now, do you think you will be okay in here for a few minutes while I get Doc? You won't try to run again?"

All I could do was nod. He'd said a lot in the past few minutes and I tried to take it all in. He couldn't be real. As I watched him stand up and walk to the door, a thought occurred to me.

"Wait!"

"What, sweetness?" Micah looked over his shoulder at me, eyebrows raised.

"What's the BRB?"

"Sweetness, the BRB is your family now. We're the Broken Rebel Brotherhood." And then, he actually winked at me.

7

MICAH

*J*esus. Sadie was going to be the death of me. I tried to reign my temper in because I knew that's not what she needed right then, but dammit, all I really wanted to do was find this Ian character and make him suffer. Oh, I knew she hadn't said it was Ian that did this to her, but I could tell she was afraid of him. What else, or who else, could it have been?

As I walked through the main house in search of Doc, I thought back to my conversation with Gram a little bit ago. I was so grateful to have figured out who the woman in my bed was, but having that information now added a new worry. How would Gram handle this new twist in her life? She was a strong woman, but ever since Pap died, I felt responsible for her. I had no idea if Sadie would be around long or even if she remembered Gram.

I reached the library, where I knew Doc would be, and opened the door. Doc sat in the overstuffed chair and poured through medical books. As a former Army medic, Doc certainly had plenty of training and experience in trauma situations, but the more cases we took on, the more and more we came up against things he hadn't seen before. That's what he said anyway. If he was in the main house, this is where he could be found.

"How's the patient?" Doc asked as he lifted his attention from the book to me.

"Sadie. Her name is Sadie."

"She's talking. That's great! You think it's her real name?"

I hated to burst his bubble but… "No, it's not great. She didn't voluntarily give it to me. She's talking, but not really saying much, ya know?"

"Okay. Care to enlighten me? How the hell do you already know her name? And why haven't we called the cops yet?"

"I've been keeping Jackson in the loop. I'll let him know this latest development soon. And I confirmed her name through my Gram."

"The hell you say!" Doc's temper was rising. He didn't like secrets and I didn't blame him. I didn't know his full story. We hadn't served together or anything and hadn't met until he came to the BRB looking for a place to belong. What I did know was that he had had a rough childhood and some shit went down between his mother and father and it ended very badly for all involved. He'd talk when he was ready. I'd learned over the course of my time in the Seals, and with the BRB, that sometimes people just didn't like to share.

"Calm down, Doc. Once you cleaned her up, I thought I recognized her. I had to confirm my suspicions before telling anyone. My Gram and Pap fostered her for a year, before my Pap died. I'd never actually met her and only saw her from a distance at Pap's funeral, so when I saw her, I didn't know for sure that it was her. It took a bit for me to figure out where I'd seen her before. I just talked to Gram and sent her a picture and she confirmed it. Right now, I just need you to get your ass in that room and check on her. She ripped out some of her stitches again and I know she's gotta be hurting.

I caught her trying to leave and you and I both know we can't let that happen. At least not until we know what happened to her. We need to keep her safe and part of that is making sure that she heals. Can you do that? Can you go check on her without scaring her to death or losing your temper?"

"Yeah, Mic. I can do that. I don't mean to question you. It just kills me to see someone like her. I detest secrets and I detest fucking abusers even more. I just want to help her. We all do. I'll go back in there and see to her stitches and whatever else she might need. After that though, I think it's time we got everyone together to discuss a plan of action. Something tells me this isn't going to be wrapped up any time soon. And if the look that just crossed your face is any indication, you won't be letting her leave any time soon. You need to get that shit locked down. She's in no position to do anything or even trust anyone right now. Least of all a bunch of broken veterans with PTSD and hair-trigger tempers. No disrespect."

He was right. I knew he was right. But when I realized who she was, the protectiveness that welled up inside of me was overwhelming. Knowing that she was someone who meant so much to my Gram made that feeling bubble over. As I walked out of the library, Doc on my heels, I pulled out my phone and sent Griffin a text.

Meeting in the library in an hour. Gather everyone.

As Vice President, Griffin would make it happen. He'd been handling everything for the week I'd been sitting vigil with Sadie. I put my phone back in my pocket, took a deep breath, and kept walking.

8

IAN

It had been a week since that bitch had got away. I had no clue how she got a car, but I'd find out. I needed to find her. She had too many injuries and I knew I wouldn't be able to explain them away like I did the one and only time she had called the police on me. Stupid fucks had actually believed she'd fallen down the stairs.

If I had competent employees, I wouldn't be stuck in Indianapolis finalizing the merger, rather than back in Pennsylvania searching for Sadie. Normally I enjoyed my time here. I'd spend most of it at the apartment while barking orders via conference call. I rarely went to the office while here but this time I had to and that pissed me off.

I'd been coming here one week a month since I was handed the reins of the company when I turned thirty. This was our second largest region and made my family a lot of money, so I had to make my presence felt. I had an apartment because I hated hotels. Sadie didn't know about the apartment because I handled the money. And as of a year ago, I had a nice side piece of ass that didn't make me insane and who knew her way around a cock. Sadie was good, but this woman was fucking magnificent.

I walked through the expensive cars I had hand-picked for the display room. I'd first met Sadie in a showroom just like this when she was nineteen and my father had hired her. She had been painfully shy, not my type, but her body had tempted me. When my father instructed me to train her, I'd jumped at the opportunity, hoping it would result in her sharing my bed.

Growing up I had a dark side, but I kept it hidden. I had learned to control the beast inside of me because I knew if I didn't, I would be beaten by my father. When Sadie and I started dating, my father put pressure on me to move out of his house, marry, have children, and continue his legacy. So, I did. Sadie and I got married and then everything changed. I suddenly felt the need to control, possess. It overtook me. I no longer lived under my father's roof and my mother had been dead for a long time. I no longer had a reason to hide my true self. My marriage unleashed the beast.

I was able to control Sadie by withholding affection or yelling at her. Growing up in foster homes, she'd already been molded to react the way I wanted. But one night she started to fight back. Only verbally, but that hadn't mattered. I backhanded her and the euphoria that flooded my system was like a drug. From that point forward, I craved that feeling and used whatever means necessary to get it. It got to the point where that feeling was harder to obtain, so I started getting more and more violent. Anything to feel that high. Occasionally Sadie would put up a fight, but that only made me more bloodthirsty.

Enough of that shit. I had to get my head back in the game. Make this merger happen so I could go back to finding Sadie. In the meantime, I'd do my goddamn job and then get my dick wet with the one woman I'd found who liked it as rough as I did.

9

SADIE

How long was I going to have to lie here? I desperately wanted to sleep, but I also wanted to flee. Decisions, decisions. Since I wasn't stupid, despite how hard Ian had tried to convince me otherwise, I'd stay. At least until I was healed enough to drive out of here without the fear of crashing again riding shotgun. But I wouldn't sleep. Not yet, anyway. Fuck, I just wanted to sleep.

I heard them before I saw them. Since opening my eyes bigger than slits took so much effort, I didn't even try.

"She's sleeping. I don't want to wake her."

"She's not sleeping," I mumbled.

Someone chuckled and it didn't sound like it came from Micah. It wasn't as deep as I imagined Micah's chuckle would be.

"Okay sweetness. You're awake. Are you up for Doc checking you over?" Ahh, there was that voice. I opened my eyes because I'd be damned if I was going to not watch what these men were doing. I didn't want to be taken by surprise.

Watching the other man as he strode over to the bed, recognition flashed. He was the man that had filled my IV.

Micah had called him 'Doc'. I had expected an actual doctor, white coat and all. Certainly not a six foot hulk of a man covered in tattoos, wearing black jeans and a leather vest with patches on it, similar to Micah's. 'Doc' was stitched in blue on the vest. He had a scar above his right eye and a full beard. His hair was cut close to his head and was the whitest blond I'd ever seen. Who were these guys? Doc turned his back to me, leaned down to get something out of the black bag sitting at his feet, and that's when I noticed the other stitching in the back of the vest. It was an eagle with its wings spread and an American Flag as a backdrop.

"What's with the vests?" I asked.

"Sweetness, they aren't vests. They're cuts. And I'll explain all of that to you later. Can Doc check you out? Please?"

I waved my hand in the air and hoped I appeared calm and careless. "Sure, why not? I'm assuming he's seen it all already. But I have one question for you, Doc."

"What's that?" Doc asked me. He seemed shy, and a bit uncomfortable. Well, that made two of us!

"Are you really a doctor? I get the impression that Doc is a name and not a title."

Rather than getting angry, he chuckled. "Yes. I really am a doctor. Former Army medic, actually. My name isn't Doc, but that's what they call me. My name is Madoc. Would you like to see my ID? My medical license?"

"No, that won't be necessary, Madoc." He tried to hide it, but I caught the slight grin at hearing his actual name. Everyone else might have called him Doc, but I thought I'd use his given name. It suited him.

"Okay. And what should I call you? Big guy over here," he jerked his thumb to indicate Micah, "has called you Red, but says that your name is Sadie."

"Sadie. You can call me Sadie." I chewed my bottom lip as I said this. I didn't really want anyone knowing my real name. Someone might talk, but something told me to trust Madoc. The jury was still out on Micah, but Madoc had gotten me through the last week so he'd earned a bit of that trust.

"Okay...Sadie." Something flashed in his eyes. Something that looked a lot like pity. I wanted to call him out on it, but I hadn't had the strength for it. The conversation had really worn me out. I tried to cover up my yawn, but I guess I hadn't done a good job.

"Okay, sweetness. We should let Doc do his thing so you can get some sleep."

"Okay," I whispered. I wasn't trying to be difficult. I really wasn't. But I was trying to reclaim a little bit of the person I knew I once was and part of that meant a little attitude. I slowly closed my eyes as Madoc walked the rest of the way to the bed and began his work.

"Did you tell her?" I heard Madoc ask as he reinserted the IV and I felt something cold pulse through my veins. I tried to follow the conversation, but I felt myself slipping away.

"Not yet," Micah answered.

Haven't told me what?

That was my last thought before sleep took over.

~

Micah

I knew the second the sedative took effect because Sadie's whole body relaxed. I sat on the other side of the bed from where Doc had been working. I picked up her hand and held it in my lap. I needed the contact. I hoped she did too.

"Why didn't you tell her?" Doc asked me.

"What do you mean why, *Madoc?*" I countered with a smirk.

"Telling her my name was just a small way I could earn her trust. She needs to know that she can talk to us and that we won't lie to her. What do you care?" Doc was frustrated, I could tell, so I moved on.

"I don't care. And I didn't tell her because I'm trying to figure out how." Doc was the only one who knew that Sadie had been a foster child in placement with my grandparents. The rest would find out at our meeting a little later.

"She deserves to know. We can't keep secrets from her. At least not this."

"I'll tell her. Once she wakes up and can handle more than a few minutes of conversation."

Doc was right, but I needed to figure out how to tell her first. I was worried that telling her she had lived with my grandparents would not be welcome news to her. I mean, she ran from there. And at a time when my Gram needed less heartache, not more.

"Fair enough. Okay, I think I'm done here. I'll leave you alone with her."

"How long will the sedative last, do you think?"

"I don't know. About six hours or so. At least, that's what I'm hoping. She needs to get as much rest as possible. On the other hand, she needs to start eating. I know we've been pushing fluids, but she can't exist on that much longer. She lost so much blood and while she's on the mend, she's not out of the woods quite yet. She's lost a few pounds in the last week. I'd say we let her sleep as long as she can, but if it goes much past dinner time, we need to wake her up and get some soup in her. It's a little after noon now, so how about we wake her up, if she's not already, around eight? Sound good?"

"Yeah. Yeah that sounds good. Don't worry about sending Nell in. She can talk to her after we get her to eat."

Doc nodded and gathered up the medical supplies all over the room before he quietly slipped out the door.

I looked down at Sadie and decided to clean up a bit. The medical supplies were gone, but there was fresh blood on the sheets from when she'd panicked. I walked to the closet in the attached bathroom and pulled out some fresh sheets. Nothing fancy, but they were clean. I looked around the room and decided that the easiest thing would be to roll her from side to side as I changed the sheets. The less I could disturb her, the better, and I was afraid that picking her up would rip out the stitches again. I couldn't bear the thought of having to watch Doc stitch up that pretty skin again.

I gently rolled Sadie as I stripped the blood and sweat stained sheets from the bed. I tossed them in the corner until I got a chance to throw them down the laundry chute. I rolled her again as I tried to put the clean sheets on the bed. She moaned a little with each roll, but she didn't wake up. Once that was done, I wasn't sure what to do. I had told the crew to meet me in the library, but I didn't want to leave her. I knew I had to, though. I assured myself that she was truly asleep, and that she'd be here when I got back, before I turned and walked out the door.

10

MICAH

*V*oices were booming as I approached the library. There was some laughter mixed in, but as soon as I opened the door and crossed the threshold, silence took over and everyone stared at me.

"How is she?"

"Is she awake?"

"Has she told you anything?"

A million questions came at me at once. I threw my hands up to signal for quiet and it worked.

Silence.

"She did wake up. She hasn't said much, at least not about what happened. She's still got a long road ahead of her, and we are going to help her walk that road. Now, let's talk about club business real quick so I can get caught up on the last week. Then we'll discuss Sadie. Aiden, care to start?" I turned to Aiden and watched as he unfolded himself from the windowsill and walked to the center of the room. There wasn't a lot of seating in the library, but it was a big room and we kind of landed where we could.

"Sure. So, I took on a case on Monday. A twenty-three-year-old woman who has a stalker. She claimed she doesn't know who it could be, but she's hiding something. I'm not sure what, but I'm working on it. Her name's Scarlett. Pretty little thing. She's holed up in my cabin with Sully for now, and I'll stay here in my room at the main house. I've invited her to dinner here with us, but she's skittish. Not ready to leave the cabin. I'll try again tomorrow." The whole time Aiden talked he had a faraway look on his face, but I let it pass. We were all under a lot of pressure right now so I chalked it up to stress and lack of sleep.

"Sounds like you got it covered. I'm glad Sully is with her. That dog is ninety pounds of pure muscle and I'm sure he makes her feel a little safer." Sully was Aiden's boxer. Aiden was a dog handler in the military and when he lost his partner overseas, he had sworn he'd never get another dog. When he returned to the States, he had found Sully and it was love at first sight. Sully was our starter stud and now Aiden had ten boxers that he was training to work with veterans with PTSD, and another litter on the way. "I'll go over and introduce myself later. Maybe the more of us she meets, the more comfortable she'll feel. Thanks for handling it. Any other business we need to discuss?"

Doc piped up. "Yeah. I'd like to discuss medical equipment, as in, we need more." He looked like it pained him to speak, but he did. He was coming out of his shell a little more and that was a good thing.

"Okay. Aiden, where do we stand with money?" I didn't know much but if Doc said we needed more medical equipment, we should see what we could do.

"We can definitely make it work. With the income from my dogs, Griff's side computer jobs, and Brie's self-defense classes, we've got plenty of money coming in. Not to mention the money we started out with."

We all brought money into the club with us. We had

earned a lot in the military and had never had anything to spend it on. I also had my inheritance from when my parents died that I had barely touched.

Aiden continued, "And with the donations we receive from past victims and the community, we aren't hurting. What're you thinking we need?"

"Nell, Doc? Can you two get together over the next few days and make a list? Between the two of you and Aiden we can start shopping around and get some stuff delivered." Nell's gaze landed on me when she heard her name. She was shocked but I just nodded and smiled at her. She had been talking about taking classes and possibly going on to medical school, so I wanted to include her in this.

"Sure, no problem boss." This from Nell. She could barely contain her excitement. Aiden and Doc chuckled at her and a blush rose up her neck. Huh. Not something I saw a lot from Nell. She was plain, and not very outspoken, but not much fazed her. She could best be described as the classic girl next door, until you got to know her.

"That's not all I need from you, Nell. Sadie is going to need some clothes and things. I also want her to see the doctor in town." I turned to Doc. "Not that I don't trust you Doc, but maybe Sadie will open up a little more to a woman." I returned my attention to Nell. "When she's feeling up to it, would you take her into town to get some things and be sure she sees the doctor?"

"I can do that," Nell responded.

"Now, let's get down to the reason I called this meeting," I said, addressing the room at large. "As you know, we have a name—Sadie. But I had suspicions that I had seen her before, and I confirmed those earlier today."

"What the fuck?" Aiden demanded. The others grumbled, but they kept their mouths shut.

"I wanted to confirm what I thought before saying

anything. Anyway," I said, pulling my fingers through my hair, "after I went into the military, my grandparents became foster parents. I guess they missed having a bratty teenager around." I paused and hoped that they would laugh at my attempt at humor, but they didn't. "They wanted to open their home to a child that needed some love and care." I spent the next few minutes telling them about Sadie being a foster child placed with my Gram and Pap, my Pap's death and how Sadie took off in the middle of the funeral. "Gram and I tried to find her but as you know, leave doesn't last forever and I had to get back. I never had the opportunity to officially meet Sadie, but I saw her from a distance at the funeral. I sent a picture of the woman in my bed to Gram and she confirmed that it was indeed Sadie."

I paused, breathed deeply and continued. "We have to find the bastard that did this to her. Not just for her, but for my Gram. Gram loved her like a daughter. Still does. And the stories Gram would tell me about the girl living in their home, well, they don't jive with the battered woman we found. I need to find out what happened to her after she left."

Griffin had been suspiciously quiet, but he spoke up now. "We were actually talking about that before you came in. I think it might work in our favor that you recognized her. Maybe we can use that to our advantage and get her to trust you because of it. In the meantime, I'm not so sure it's a good idea to jump right into tracking down the pussy that did this to her. We agree that there's more than just the wreck to consider, but until we have more information, we need to be careful. We don't know what we're dealing with." I narrowed my eyes at Griffin and let my frustration show. "Think about it, Micah. No matter what the mission or who the victim is, we always plan. Gather as much intel as we can before acting. We need to do that now. I know this is more than just a job for you, but you need to keep that in check. It's the only way."

"You're right. I know you're right. But I don't like it." Deep breath. "Okay. So how about this. We take the next few weeks and let Sadie heal. I'll explain to her who I am and hopefully get to know her. See if I can get her to open up about what happened. In the meantime, I also want to be doing some of that research. Griffin, once we have a full name, I want you tracking down this Ian asshole she keeps mentioning and find out everything about him. Where he works, what his schedule is, who he hangs out with, his strengths, his weaknesses. Hell, I want to know what brand of tighty-whities he wears and how many times he takes a dump a day. Every. Damn. Thing."

"Sure."

"Hell, yeah."

"We can do that."

The voices rang out as they all agreed.

We talked for a few more minutes until it seemed we'd talked our meager plan to death. Time to get back to Sadie. I'd only been away from her for about an hour, but I needed to see her. I needed to see that she was still there, in my bed.

"Anything else?" Everyone shook their heads. "Okay then. Meeting adjourned." Everyone filed out of the library. Griffin would start trying to dig up some information. He was great with computers and our go-to guy for that stuff. Aiden would look at the finances to see where we stood and how much we could afford for the medical equipment. Doc was on kitchen duty, so he'd be making dinner and Nell was on watch. That only left Brie. I hadn't seen her leave. In fact, I didn't recall her saying anything during the entire meeting. Frowning, I turned back to the room and there she was, sitting on the windowsill, staring at nothing out the big picture window.

"Brie. What's up?"

"Nothing. It's nothing." Brie shrugged before slowly

standing and turning toward me. Interesting. She hadn't meant a word she had just said.

"You know you can talk to me, right? To any of us." I walked toward her as I was talking and stopped when I was a few feet away. Brie stared at the floor and avoided my gaze.

"Kiddo, talk to me. What's wrong?" I was really worried about her, but like everyone else, she'd talk when she was ready. This was the last time I'd ask.

"I'm okay. Honestly. Just…" She trailed off leaving that thought hanging.

"Just what?"

"Just don't hurt her, okay? I can see the way you look at her. I can tell you have feelings for her. She's been through hell and she needs love and care. She doesn't need a big, bad veteran slash biker swooping in to take care of everything. She needs you to stand beside her. I promise you, she's stronger than you think. Probably stronger than she gives herself credit for. You can take care of her and stand beside her, but don't for one second keep her in the dark about what's going on. That won't help her."

Wow. That was a lot.

"I can do that. I don't want to hurt her. And between you and me, yes, I have feelings for her. I want to protect her. I can't explain it, but she makes me feel…something."

Brie's mascara had started to run but she'd never admit she was crying. Instead, she turned her head and discretely wiped the tears off her face. When she turned back, she smiled slightly.

"Thank you. Can I go now? All this mushy girly stuff is not my thing." She punched me on the arm as she said this, and I threw my head back and laughed. God, it felt good to laugh.

"Yeah, you can go. See you at dinner?"

"Maybe. Not sure if I'm going out with Zach or not." Not what I wanted to hear, but I let it go…for now.

As Brie walked out of the library, I couldn't help but feel a little zing whip though my system at the thought of seeing Sadie again. Then I heard a scream.

11

SADIE

I tossed and turned as the nightmare worsened.

"Goddamnit, Sadie! How could you let this happen?"

"How could I let this happen? It takes two to make a baby, Ian. I didn't knock myself up."

I thought he'd be happier at the news of my pregnancy. We never really talked about having kids, but we never talked about not having them either. Yelling at him was stupid but sometimes he made me so angry that I couldn't stop myself. I guessed that the punishment for my outburst would be brutal, but maybe not. Maybe he'd take into consideration that I was pregnant.

"I know that, you ignorant little cunt! But I thought you were on the pill." He grabbed my hair and yanked my head back while he was talking, "Did you do this on purpose?"

"No," I wailed, "I don't know how it happened. I always take my pill, you know that."

"I don't believe you," he thundered.

"I don't care," I spat at him.

After he swiped his hand down his face to clean it, his eyes sparked, and his face became an angry shade of red. He dragged me *toward the phone on the wall, the one that no longer worked because Ian had had our service cut off a year ago. Next thing I knew, he wrapped the phone cord around my neck. He'd never done anything before that would leave a visible mark, so I was too stunned to fight back.*

"Fucking bitch! You did this to yourself, ya know? It's your own fault I have to do this to you." A wicked smile appeared on his face and my blood ran cold.

"I'm so...so...sorry, Ian," I wailed. When did I become this person? This person who begged and pleaded just to be shown a little human kindness. From my husband, no less.

Ian loosened the cord around my neck, and I sucked in as much oxygen as I could. Before I could catch my breath, he had his arm locked under my chin and dragged me out of the kitchen, toward the basement stairs. Ian threw open the door and started to drag me downstairs. My legs bounced off each step and I knew my legs would be covered in bruises. Bruises that no one would see. I didn't understand why he was taking me downstairs. He'd never done this before. This was the most violent he'd ever gotten.

We reached the bottom of the rickety wooden steps and Ian slammed me down on my back on the concrete floor. Whatever breath I had left whooshed out of me. I started to cough and for that, I got a kick to the gut.

"Get on your knees." The evil smile was back as he reached for his belt, undid it and his dress pants and pushed them both to his knees. I lay there, too stunned to comply. Another kick to the gut. "I said, get on your fucking knees!"

I scramble to my knees to obey. As soon as I'm in the position he wanted he grabbed my jaw roughly with one hand, making it impossible for me to keep my mouth closed, and with the other hand he grabbed his dick, guiding it as he rammed it home. Silent tears streamed down my face and I did everything in my power not to move, not to gag. He found release in a few quick thrusts and then shoved me back to the floor.

He's out of his mother fucking mind, I thought, watching him pull his pants up and smiling like the Cheshire Cat. I tried to sit up, but I couldn't, so I curled up into a ball and tried to get my crying under control. Out of the corner of my eye, I saw Ian put a bucket about five feet away from me and then he started toward the stairs. I wondered what the bucket was for, but Ian didn't seem inclined to tell me and I wasn't going to ask. He'd never leave me down here long enough to need to use it.

"Where are you going?" I couldn't stop the clawing fear that he was going to leave me down here by myself. Stupid, I know, after all he'd done, but for some strange reason, I still loved him. He was all I had in this world. He'd made sure of that.

"None of your fucking business. I'll be gone for a while, so make yourself comfy." That sounded so...evil. Ian walked up the stairs and then the light blinked out. The lock engaged on the door, and I knew I wouldn't be getting out of there until Ian decided to let me out. As I listened to his footsteps on the hardwood floor above me and then the opening and closing of the door to the garage, I resigned myself to a few hours of hell. Because that's what it would be down here in the dark. Hell. Then, I remembered the reason he had dragged me down here in the first place and screamed.

∾

Micah

I'd never forget that scream. When I heard it, my blood boiled. It wasn't like I was far from the bedroom, but it felt like it took a lifetime to get there.

When I reached the door, the screaming intensified. It didn't sound human. It sounded like a banshee had taken up residence in my bed where I had left a flesh and blood woman. I threw open the door and stopped dead in my tracks. Sadie was trying to flail her arms and legs, but the twisting of the sheet around her body made it almost impossible. I'd had nightmares before and I knew I shouldn't touch her, but I needed her to stop before she hurt herself.

I reached the bed in four long strides and tried to grab Sadie's arms to pin them down. I knew it might hurt her, but not as bad as she'd be hurting if I let this continue.

"Sadie! Sadie! It's just a dream. Wake up, sweetness." I tried to get her attention, but it didn't work.

"Sweetness. Hey, hey, hey. It's me. It's Micah. You need to wake up now." I said this over and over until finally she began to calm. I watched as her eyes slowly opened and some focus seeped into her gaze. Her beautiful forget-me-not blue gaze.

"Micah?"

"Yeah, sweetness. It's me. Bad dream?"

"Um, yeah, I guess you could say that." Her eyes focused on her wringing hands. I knew that if she looked at me, I'd see the fear, the terror. I hadn't wanted to see it, but I needed her to know that she could show it to me.

"Sweetness, can you look at me? Can you talk about it?"

"I...I...I don't know. It's not a pretty story, Micah." She sounded so small in that moment. I wanted to wrap her up in my arms and promise her the world.

"Okay. How about this? Are you hungry? Doc's made some dinner and I think he made you some soup. You haven't eaten in a while and should probably try. After dinner, if you're feeling up to it, we can talk." At the mention of food, her eyes lit up, and I heard the faintest of grumbling coming from her belly. Ahh, so my girl liked to eat. I'd have to keep that in mind.

"I guess so. Soup sounds good. Um, Micah?"

"Yeah, Sadie?"

"Can I eat here? I'm...I'm not ready to face everyone yet." I hated the halting in her voice, but I understood it.

"I can bring your food in here. Can I eat with you?" I held my breath while I waited for her answer.

"I think I can handle that. But if…" She let that thought trail from her lips unfinished. I had a pretty good idea what she was worried about, so I tried to ease her mind.

"Sweetness, if at any point you don't feel comfortable, you just tell me and I'll leave."

"Okay. Thank you."

"Anytime, sweetness. Anytime."

12

SADIE

After Micah had pulled me from my nightmare, it took me a while to calm down. My knee-jerk reaction was to be afraid of him, but there was something about him that quieted my fears. Maybe it was his patience. He never pushed and he always seemed to sense what I needed before I could fully explain it to myself, let alone out loud.

After I had agreed to try and eat some soup, Micah had left me alone to rest, only after having reassured himself I'd be okay. I insisted I would be fine, but now I wondered if I was wrong. Now that he wasn't here, I felt the panic setting in. *What is going on with me?* After what I had so recently escaped, I couldn't believe I was relying on another man again. Not only that, but I *liked* it. Liked him.

Craziness! I was a shell of the girl I once was. I shouldn't be wasting my time on fanciful thoughts of a man who was just giving me a place to lay my head for a bit. I realized I was probably grasping at any hint of kindness and I wanted to latch on and never let go, but I couldn't. Not now. Maybe not ever.

Since dinner wasn't for another hour or so and I wasn't in

as much pain since I'd done nothing but sleep and dream in the last week, I decided to take a shower. Micah had told me he'd left me a washcloth and towel on the bathroom sink, so I gingerly got up and walked toward the bathroom. As I pushed open the door, the overwhelming urge to get clean crashed into me. I walked a little faster and when I reached the shower I leaned over and turned on the hot water. I knew it'd probably burn but cold water couldn't possibly wash the ugliness away.

I took off the sweats and t-shirt that Micah had given me to wear and gently stepped over the edge of the tub and under the hot spray. It felt glorious. I grabbed the shampoo and squirted a generous amount into the palm of my hand and then lathered it into my hair. As I rinsed the suds from my head, I watched as it swirled in the bottom of the tub in a mass of brown and red-tinged bubbles. I knew that Micah had said that he had Nell, I thought that was her name, give me sponge baths, but clearly there had been no way to get all the blood and grime off me.

After I finished cleaning my hair, I picked up the bar of Ivory soap and lathered it onto the washcloth. I started scrubbing my body, and suddenly, I couldn't stop. I couldn't scrub hard enough or long enough. Everything...every foster home move, every beating, every put-down, every emotion came flooding into my memory and I lost it. I leaned back against the wall and slid down to the floor of the tub. I drew my knees up to my chest and clutched them as tight as I could, afraid that somehow, if I let go, another part of me would be lost. I was sobbing and I couldn't stop. I didn't know if I'd ever be able to stop.

∽

Micah

I had left Sadie about an hour ago. I had checked on Doc to see if he needed any help with dinner and exchanged texts with Brie. I'd gone with Aiden to his cabin to meet Scarlett. After talking to her for a while and assuring her that she'd be safe here, I'd come back to the main house. I was running out of things to do, so I gave up the fight and started toward my room.

As I walked into the bedroom four things immediately hit me. First, Sadie wasn't in the bed. Second, the shower was running. Third, there was an unnatural amount of steam coming out through the crack of the bathroom door. And fourth...the fourth thing was what tore me up inside...there was the unmistakable sound of sobbing coming from the bathroom and it sounded like it was coming from someone who was having their soul ripped right out of their chest.

I rushed through the bathroom door and yanked open the shower curtain. Sadie was on the floor, curled up as tight as I imagined she could get. I crouched down next to the tub and took in the sight before me, trying to quickly gather my thoughts because I was pissed. Pissed that someone as beautiful as Sadie was dealing with this. Pissed that evil existed in the world. Pissed that I couldn't fix it. Once I was sure I wouldn't scare her, or at least as sure as I could be, I reached out to her. She flinched as my hands got close, so I turned off the water to buy her a second to get used to me being near.

"Sweetness, it's okay. You're going to be okay. I promise." I didn't know why I was promising her that because it sure as shit wasn't okay, but I would do everything in my power to make sure that it was.

"I...I...co...co...couldn't get cl...cl...clean," she sobbed. That was when I noticed how red her body was. Judging by the temperature of the water and the grip she had on the washcloth, she'd tried hard to wash the brutal memories away. How could I tell her it didn't work like that? That no amount of hot water and scrubbing would erase her pain?

"Sweetness, I'm going to help you get out of the tub. Is that okay? Can I help you out of the tub?"

Sadie didn't answer me, so I took a chance and scooped her up in my arms and carried her back to the bed, leaving a trail of water as I went. I gently placed her on the mattress and risked a few seconds away from her to grab a towel. Once I returned to the bed, Sadie was still crying, so I started to methodically dry her off. She didn't fight me on it, so I considered it a win.

Once I had her body dry, I went back into the bathroom and grabbed my comb off the counter. I took the time to comb out Sadie's wet, tangled hair. While I was doing that, her crying slowed and became more of a wet hiccupping.

Once her hair was free of tangles, I took the wet towel and comb back to the bathroom and dropped the whole mess on the floor. I could clean up later. When I walked back into the bedroom, Sadie was gripping the sheet on the bed in an effort to cover her breasts. I wouldn't tell her that covering herself would never erase the picture of her breasts I had in my head. I couldn't un-see that if I tried. Perfect pillow-like breasts with big rosy nipples. Without all the blood to obscure the view, I could look at her creamy complexion for hours and never tire of seeing it, of seeing her. Count the freckles that scattered across her body. My dick twitched and I prayed to God she couldn't tell.

"Micah?" Sadie's voice broke me from my traitorous thoughts.

"Hmm?" With the picture of her naked body running unfiltered through my head, that was the best I could manage. I shifted slightly to get more comfortable. Not an easy task with the bulge in my pants.

"I'm hungry." I could tell she hadn't wanted to make that

admission, like it somehow made her weak or lessened what had just happened.

I chuckled. "Okay, sweetness. You're in luck. I think dinner is about ready. What do you want to wear? I've got some more sweats you can throw on. Or I can see if Nell has anything that will fit you. Or you could stay in your birthday suit." Her eyes widened and then I heard the most beautiful sound. She laughed.

13

SADIE

As I sat on the bed and ate my soup, I tried to come up with something to say. Micah had brought his dinner and a chair into the bedroom and he sat next to the bed, quietly eating. I couldn't take the silence any longer.

"So, um, tell me something about you," I said.

"What do you want to know?" he asked around a bite of his steak. I envied him that steak but understood why the soup was the better bet.

"Well, I know your name is Micah. But that's about it. You mentioned the BRB, I think you called it. What exactly is that?"

"That's an easy one. The BRB is the Broken Rebel Brotherhood. We're a motorcycle club and we have a passion for helping people. We're all veterans. I'm not saying we are paragons of virtue or anything because, shit, we all have our demons and crosses to bear. But we try to always do what's right. Our specialty is helping victims of domestic violence. In fact, not too long before we found you, we finished up a case. And right now…right now we have a woman on our property who has a stalker. Aiden's handling that situation while I help you. Now, my turn."

"Wait, no. I have a few more questions."

"And you'll get to ask them, but I think it's only fair that you answer a question first," he argued.

"Fine, ask away," I said because it didn't seem worth the argument.

"What's your full name?"

"Damn, jump right in, why don't you?" It's not like I couldn't tell him, but I thought I'd have more time.

"Sweetness, I could easily find out the information, but I'm asking you instead. So, what's your full name?"

"Sadie Harper McCord." I purposely looked away and mumbled my married name. I hoped he wouldn't catch it.

"Hmm... why the hesitation with 'McCord'?" Shit, he hadn't missed it.

"Because that's my married name and I'm not ready to talk about that yet." I winced at his raised eyebrows and immediately wished I could call back the words or at least that I had said them with less venom. "My turn. What does that tattoo mean?" I asked pointing to the one on his right forearm. It looked familiar somehow and was bugging the shit out of me.

"It's my family crest. I got it after my Pap passed away." His gray eyes darkened slightly as he spoke, and I almost felt bad for asking. Almost. "I've got others, but that's the most important one."

"It looks familiar to me, but I don't know why. I mean, why would it? I don't know you." I was talking more to myself at this point. I was confused and I didn't like the feeling. He'd known my first name before I even gave it to him. "How'd you know my name?" I demanded. No matter how hard I tried, I kept circling back to that fact.

"Which question do you want answered first?" His brows raised as he looked at me expectantly.

"My name. How'd you know my name?"

He took a deep breath before speaking. "I guess this is as good a time as any to tell you."

"Tell me what?" My head snapped up to stare into his eyes. I wasn't sure I wanted to know but at the same time, I had to know.

"You know my name is Micah, but you don't know my last name." He looked hesitant to continue. "Mallory. My name is Micah Mallory." His eyes searched mine, looking for something, although I couldn't tell what.

"That doesn't answer my—" My mouth snapped shut as his last name registered. "Did you say Mallory?"

"Yes."

"And you were in the military?"

"Yes."

"Oh my God! You're their grandson! Sylvia and Clay, they were...they were the last foster parents I ever lived with." Everything clicked into place. Tears started to stream down my face because I hadn't thought about the couple who opened their hearts to me in a long time.

"I am. I had left for the military by the time you were placed with them and we never actually met. I wanted to meet the girl Gram always gushed about in her emails, but when I went to introduce myself to you at Pap's funeral, I couldn't find you. You were gone. We looked for you, Gram and I, for a few days but you were gone. Why? Why did you leave?"

"I had to," I cried, the tears poured down my cheeks unchecked. Micah brought his thumbs up to my face and I flinched. He halted for a split second before he wiped the tears away.

"Why?" he breathed.

"Micah, there's no easy way to answer that question. I'll try though." I began to tell him a little of my history. "It all started with Shawn."

"Who the fuck is Shawn?" Micah interrupted.

"He was my baby brother," I snapped, not liking his tone. "He died of SIDS when he was five months old."

"Oh God, I'm sorry. I didn't know. Gram never said you had a brother."

"They didn't know. No one knew. I never talked about him because it hurt too bad." The ache in my chest grew, as it always did when I thought of Shawn. "His funeral was the first of many." I looked down at my hands and realized they had turned white from wringing them so tightly.

"What's 'many'?"

"Twelve, including Clay's. The second and third were for my parents, who turned to drugs to handle their grief. It didn't end well. My father overdosed and my mother shot herself while high. Escaping from their hell ensured that I lived in a worse hell for the next fourteen years." I chanced a look at him and was surprised by what I saw. It wasn't the pity I was expecting and had gotten so used to, but rather… admiration. "The other nine funerals were of relatives of foster parents and after each one, I was moved to a new home. I had become so numb to the pain of loss that I just quit crying. It didn't bring people back and it didn't make foster parents want to keep me."

"Jesus. I had no idea. Why didn't you tell my grandparents? They could have helped you deal with some of this. You weren't alone anymore." Micah made it sound so easy, but it hadn't been. Nothing about my life after Shawn had been easy.

"I was sixteen when I was first brought to them. Sixteen, Micah. Do you remember what it was like to be sixteen? Teenagers are bratty and difficult and those are the ones with good lives, with loving homes. I had neither. I fought their kindness as much as I could. In every way I could. I failed miserably at that, and eventually, they won me over." I smiled at the memory. "Clay broke down my defenses after I skipped school one day. I showed up at the house and he was waiting for me in the living room. I could tell by the look on his face that he knew, and I braced myself for a beating that never came. Instead, he won me over with a stern lecture about not skipping school that ended with him giving me a hug."

"That sounds like him," Micah said, chuckling. "I got many similar lectures and the last one ended up with me going into the military."

"After his funeral, I knew I still had Sylvia, but I believed she'd throw me away like the others had. In her grief, I thought I would become a nobody to her."

"That would never have happened," Micah insisted.

"I didn't know that, though," I said as I waved my hand around. "Anyway, I panicked. I took off because I couldn't bear the thought of Sylvia sending me away while wrapped up in her grief. I'd learned that it was easier on my heart if I didn't have to endure being tossed aside like the unwanted girl I had always been. So, I left before that could happen."

"My God, you were just a child. Where did you go?"

"I'd managed to make a few friends when I'd moved in with them and I used that to my advantage over the next year. Luckily for me, their parents didn't seem to mind having a house guest. When I graduated from high school I was on my own. All those friends I'd made started leaving for college so I couldn't stay at their houses anymore. I was able to get a job as a receptionist at the headquarters of a major car dealership in Pittsburgh and that's where…" I breathed deeply, not quite able to believe we'd managed to get to the part of the conversation I'd been dreading the most. "That's where I met Ian, my husband."

～

Micah

Surprised at her admission, I stayed quiet because she seemed to need a minute. When, after a few minutes, she still hadn't continued, I blurted the first thing that popped into my head.

"You're still married?"

"Um, yes, I am," she mumbled without looking at me.

"You're not wearing a wedding ring." I left out the fact that I had checked as soon as I was able to see her hands.

"Oh, no, I guess I'm not." She still hadn't looked at me, but she held her hand up in front of her as if noticing it for the first time. "I had one, though. I threw it out the window somewhere in Ohio while making my getaway." That's when she looked at me and changed the subject. "So, when can I leave?"

"In a hurry to get somewhere?" The words came out more gruffly than I had intended but the thought of her leaving made my gut clench.

"Yes! I'm in a hurry to get as far away from Ian as I can," she snapped, with the first spark of life I'd seen since beginning this conversation.

"You can't leave."

"And who's going to stop me?" she asked, her voice rising.

"Let me ask you something." I needed her to understand why she couldn't keep running and fast, before this conversation turned any more childish with the 'cannot, can to' bullshit. "How much money do you have?"

"What's that got to do with anything? And how is that any of your business?"

"Humor me."

"Fine. I have a little under twenty-five hundred dollars."

"Twenty-five hundred? And how far do you think that'll get you?"

"Well, I don't know but farther than here, that's for sure."

"That'll last you a few weeks, at best. If you leave, you're going to have to stay at hotels, because you can't drive nonstop. Then there's gas and food." I was pissing her off, but that was better than her being gone. "And let's not forget that you'll need a new car before any of that other stuff even comes in to play."

"Oh, God." Her hand came up to her mouth and she began to bite her nails.

"Sadie, I know you're scared and I'm sorry if I made you feel worse, but you *are* safe here, whether you realize it or not," I explained. "All of us here are trained to serve and protect. We will do whatever we have to in order to make sure you stay safe. Besides, do you really want to spend the rest of your life running? Because that's what you'll be doing if you leave. Let us help you. Let *me* help you."

"But why? What do you get out of it?"

"Why do I need to get anything out of it? Can't I simply want to help an old friend, family?" I asked.

"Micah, I'm not your friend and I'm sure as hell not family. I don't have a family." She whispered that last part.

"Aw, sweetness, the second my grandparents gave you a home, you became family. And my Gram used to write me letters about you all the time. After reading them, I kind of felt like I knew you. Those letters and stories about you made me smile at a time when I didn't think smiling was possible. For that alone, you're my friend." I paused and picked up her hand. She tried to pull it away, but I didn't let her. "Are you so afraid of Ian that you can't let yourself have a friend? Was it that bad?"

"It was bad, Micah. I can't even begin to describe how bad. I'm not ready to talk about all of that yet, but," she paused and looked at our joined hands, "you're right. Sort of. I *am* afraid of Ian and what he'll do to me if he finds me, but it's time I fight back. Reclaim the parts of me I lost over the last decade. That's why I left, after all." She took a deep breath and blew it out. "If you're sure I can stay, then I will. For now. But you have to promise me that if I want to leave, you'll let me. If I'm going to move forward, I can't feel like I'm being held hostage. Been there, done that."

"Fair enough. On one condition. If you're going to run, tell me." What I left unsaid was that I would do my damndest to convince her to stay.

"I can do that."

"Thank you." Sadie tried to hide her yawn, but I caught it. "Why don't you get some rest? Tomorrow is a new day and we can worry about everything else then."

"I think I'll take you up on that offer. I'm beat." She winced. "Poor choice of words. I am going to call it a night though, if that's okay."

"Of course it's okay." I stood and began to collect our dinner dishes. "I'll stay here at the main house as long as you're here. If you'd like more privacy, we can stay at my place when you're ready." I started for the door before I turned back around to look at her. "Good night, Sadie. Sweet dreams."

"Night, Micah."

14

SADIE

It'd been two weeks since Micah had found me and a week since my conversation with him about staying. A lot had happened since then. On Wednesday, Madoc took out my stitches and said I was healing nicely. Micah still wanted me to see a doctor in town to be sure, and while I wasn't crazy about that, Nell had bribed me with shopping and lunch, so I caved.

The doctor asked a lot of questions about how I got my injuries and I hadn't wanted to share, but she made a good case when she explained that it would be helpful to have documentation about how I received them if I ever chose to bring charges against Ian. So, I explained. And I cried. The doctor listened patiently and before we were done, she declared that Madoc was right, I was healing nicely, but she wanted to see me back in a month to check my progress. By the time I'd left, my eyes were red and puffy and I was exhausted.

Lunch and shopping with Nell were next. As we ate, we discovered we both loved french-fries dipped in chocolate milkshakes and laughed about how others thought it was weird. At the diner, Nell did most of the talking but I didn't care. It was nice to listen. For the first time in years, I felt like I had a friend.

Up until this point, we'd been having a good time. We were standing at the cash register at Target and I'd just handed over cash to pay for my purchase. Nell had followed me around, not saying much as I'd thrown random items into the cart. I hadn't bothered to try anything on because it didn't matter.

"That's the third pair of sweatpants you've bought. Girl, you can't exist in sweatpants." Nell's tone suggested she meant no offense, but her comment triggered shame to wash over me.

"That's um, all he allowed me to wear." I tucked a strand of hair behind my ear and ducked my head.

"Shit. I'm sorry." Nell's arm came around my shoulders. "I didn't mean anything by it, but—"

"It's fine." I grabbed my change from the cashier and shoved it into my pocket. I didn't want to talk about it. All that would do is remind me that I was still letting Ian control me. "I think I'm ready to go back now."

I pulled away from her but halted when her hand touched my arm. "Sadie, he's not here to tell you what to buy or what to wear. What do *you* want?"

I considered her question and after several minutes I had the answer. I squared my shoulders and stared her in the eyes. "I want to feel good. Pretty."

"Then let's go make you feel pretty." With that she tugged my arm and led me out of the store.

I didn't know where she was taking me but decided to trust her a little. We drove to the mall and she proceeded to take me to several stores that she deemed 'perfect for making a woman feel good'. I was hesitant at first, not wanting to spend my hard-earned money on frivolous clothes, but Nell

BROKEN SOULS

was persistent. She even paid for some things with her credit card, telling me to consider it a gift. A gift for what, I wasn't sure, but persistent Nell was a little overwhelming, so I relented. And I was glad I did.

I was now the proud owner of lacy lingerie in a variety of colors and styles that I'd likely never need but that made me feel sexy, as well as other various items that made me feel the same.

As we exited the mall, a tingling sensation crept up my spine. I'd been feeling like we were being watched all day and had managed to ignore it, but I couldn't any longer.

"I think we're being watched." I grabbed Nell's arm to stop her from stepping off the sidewalk into the parking lot. I looked around but didn't see anything out of the ordinary.

"Of course you do," she huffed. "Micah had Griffin follow us. I don't know why. It's not like I can't handle whatever may come up, but he's protective of you."

I didn't pursue the conversation further, but I seethed the entire way home and then all evening. When Micah walked into the house, I let him have it.

"You can't do that damnit!" I didn't bother with a greeting or pleasantries. I was too pissed. I stood toe-to-toe with him, not even caring that he towered over me.

"Do what, Sadie? I have no idea what you're talking about." His confusion sounded genuine, but it didn't matter.

"Have people watch me! I know that you thought you were protecting me, but I was jumpy all day. I felt someone watching me, and until Nell told me it was Griffin, I was scared!" I yelled.

Micah watched me with his arms crossed over his chest while I ranted and paced away from him.

"You're right. I'm sorry I didn't tell you." He followed me as I paced and stopped when he was a few inches away. "But I will not apologize for doing what I thought was necessary to ensure your safety."

"And you can dole out any punishment…" I stopped, as what he said finally registered. "Wait, did you say I was right and that you're sorry?"

"Yeah, I did." He chuckled. "I'm man enough to admit when I'm wrong, and I was wrong." Micah unfolded his arms and reached out to tuck an errant strand of hair behind my ear. I flinched but that didn't stop him. "I have a feeling you weren't expecting that. You were expecting me to get angry and lash out, weren't you?"

"Well, yeah. I mean, that's how it works." I looked down at my feet, all my bravado gone. I was that timid woman again, who did whatever Ian asked in order to avoid a beating.

"Sweetness, no. Look at me, please." I raised my eyes to his. "I will never lay a hand on you in anger. I can't promise that I'll never yell or get angry, but I'll never hurt you. No one here ever would. Do you hear me?" He paused, his eyes searching mine. "I don't know what he did to you, but your injuries speak for themselves. I'm. Not. Him."

I didn't trust myself to speak, so I just nodded. I knew it was stupid to trust again so soon, but I believed him. I didn't think Micah would hurt me, but some things were so ingrained in me that I couldn't help how I reacted. Micah had been patient with me, though.

After that, he made a point to change the subject to something less intense and we ended up talking until the early morning hours. He was really funny, and I loved hearing stories about the other BRB members. He didn't ask much more about me other than boring things like what my favorite color and food were. He seemed to sense that anything deeper than that was beyond my capability right then.

The few days since our argument had been pretty calm. During the day, Micah handled BRB business, and then he spent the evenings with me in his room. We'd talk and play cards, acting as if my world hadn't just crashed and burned. Normal stuff.

Tomorrow, I was moving into Micah's cabin and I was beyond nervous about it. Although, not for the obvious reasons. I was nervous to be alone with Micah. Not because I thought he'd hurt me, but just the opposite. I wasn't ready for a relationship. Hell, I was still married. But the way Micah flirted with me made it too easy to flirt back.

"All yours," Micah said as he exited the bathroom in nothing but a towel.

"Thanks," I mumbled. I stood rooted to the spot as I watched him disappear into his bedroom. He left the door open a crack and I stared as the towel dropped to the floor. He bent to pick it up and before he could turn around and catch me, I scurried into the bathroom and slammed the door.

So far, I'd done a good job of hiding my attraction to him but that'd be almost impossible if we were completely alone.

I mean, damn, that chest. This wasn't the first time I'd caught a glimpse of him after he'd showered. Images of him with wet tousled hair, water dripping down his smooth muscles toward the towel he always had slung at his waist, popped into my head. My hands itched to follow those droplets to their destination. That thought had my hand gliding toward my panties.

A knock on the bathroom door forced my hand to still and my breath to hitch.

"Sadie, Jackson's here. Are you almost done?" Micah's voice came through the door.

"Um, yeah. I'll be out in a minute." My voice rasped. Why'd he have to get ready so fast?

"Okay, we'll be in the kitchen." I heard his footsteps as he retreated from the room.

All of a sudden, butterflies bombarded my tummy and Micah's chest was forgotten. I was scared as hell, but Micah had assured me that I could trust Jackson. I quickly threw on my jeans and took one last look in the mirror. *Good enough.*

When I walked into the kitchen, two pairs of eyes focused on me.

"Hi." I hoped they didn't hear the breathless tone in my voice.

"Hello. I'm Jackson." He thrust his hand out to shake mine and I hesitated a split second before reaching out and allowing the contact.

"I'm Sadie." I sat at the table after shaking his hand, needing the barrier of the table to protect me. From what, I didn't know, but it made me feel better.

Jackson was friendly and had immediately put me at ease. He and Micah bantered back and forth for a few minutes, which almost made me forget why he was there. Almost.

"So, Sadie, can you tell me about what happened?" Jackson finally got down to the reason he had come.

Knowing that he and Micah were friends made spilling my guts a little easier. There were things that I left out because I hadn't felt comfortable sharing and, quite frankly, the first time I talked about the more *sexual* parts of my relationship with Ian was going to be with Micah. Jackson and Micah tried to convince me to file for a divorce, but I was so afraid it would lead Ian to me that I put it off. I had agreed to a protective order so Jackson had me fill out the necessary paperwork and told me he would file it first thing Monday morning.

"I'll be in touch as soon as Ian's served with the protective order." Jackson smiled as he talked. "In the meantime, try to relax."

Was he always so positive when someone else's life hung in the balance?

"Thanks, Sheriff. I'll try."

"Call me Jackson. We're not formal around here. Besides, you'll be seeing a lot of me if you stay around long enough." He smiled and then turned to Micah. "Walk me out? I've got a situation I want to run by you."

"Sure thing," Micah answered. "Sadie, I'll be right back."

"Take your time," I said, a little too cheerfully. Micah gave me a questioning look. *Damn*, that man didn't miss a thing. The butterflies had returned at the thought of the protective order, but I hadn't wanted them to know that.

15

MICAH

"What's up?" I asked Jackson. I wanted to go back inside and ask Sadie the same thing. Her words had said one thing, but her tone suggested something completely different.

"Nothing. I just didn't want to scare Sadie with the rest of what I had to say." We had been standing on the front porch and as Jackson talked, he looked back toward the screen door. "Pretty little thing, isn't she?"

"Beautiful."

"It's a shame she's been through so much recently. I'd ask her out in a heartbeat."

"Back the fuck off," I growled as I got right up in Jackson's face.

"Christ man," Jackson put his hands up in mock surrender. "I was kidding! C'mon, you know me better than that. It's clear that you've staked your claim whether either one of you is ready to admit it or not. Or if either of you even realizes it. I was just checking to make sure I read the situation right."

"Shit." Running my fingers through my hair, I realized Jackson had been baiting me.

"Fine. So what? I like her. It's nuts, though. I mean, I barely know her. And there are things she doesn't know about me." I chanced a look at Jackson, and he had a smirk on his face.

"Micah, I'm only going to say this once because this is getting a little too deep for a conversation between dudes, but don't be a fucking idiot. If you find someone who can make you as jealous as you just were, you need to hold onto her. Trust me. I've been where you are, and I was an idiot. I kick myself for letting *the one* get away every day. And don't worry about what she doesn't know. You'll tell her and it will be fine. If it isn't, she's not worth your jealousy."

"You make it sound so easy, but it's not." Jackson didn't know my secrets. The only people that knew were my team, my family. "Now, what did you want to talk to me about?"

"Did Sadie have a cell phone when you found her? It occurred to me that I could go through it and see if it offers any leads on this Ian prick."

"I didn't notice one. Come to think of it, she hasn't asked about that or any of her other belongings, what little there was in the car."

"Okay. You need to get her a phone and soon. I have a feeling that this protective order may bring Ian out of the woodwork and I want her to have a way to get a hold of any of us if she ever finds herself alone and in trouble."

"I'll get on it first thing in the morning. Anything else?" I was getting anxious to get back in the house.

"I want Brie to work with her on some self-defense moves and I don't think it would hurt if she learned her way around a gun."

"Already on it. I talked to Brie about that and she's going

to start working with Sadie as soon as she is feeling up to it. As for the gun, we'll get there."

"Great. The only other thing that leaves is the divorce."

"What about it?" I asked, not sure where he was going with that.

"You need to talk her into starting that process. Not only would it open up that door for you," Jackson nudged me in the arm as he said that, "but it would also go a long way toward her being completely free of him."

"Yeah, I'll add that to the list."

Jackson and I talked for a few more minutes before he left, and I went back inside to torture myself by being with a woman I wanted but couldn't have. I had to force myself to slow my walking so I didn't appear too excited when I saw her. I knocked on my bedroom door.

"Come in," Sadie called out.

I strode through the door and what I saw took my breath away. Sadie had changed from her form-fitting jeans and t-shirt to a pretty pale blue sundress.

"You changed," I said, breathing harder that I wanted her to hear. I immediately wanted to call the words back because she started to fidget with her dress.

"Oh, yeah. I wanted to look nice for dinner with everyone. Stupid, right? If you'll just give me a minute I'll change back," she said a little too quickly.

"No!" I grabbed her hands to stop her fidgeting and tried to soften my tone. "I didn't mean you looked bad. Quite the opposite. You look gorgeous. I'm just so used to seeing you in sweats or jeans that it took me by surprise."

"Really? It's okay? Not too much?" she asked shyly.

"Definitely okay. Better than okay, actually." I was going to have a hell of a time keeping my hands off of her. Heat crept up my neck at the thought. "Uh, are you hungry?

Dinner's ready." I prayed she didn't catch my unease at my thoughts. I didn't want to scare her.

"Starving." There was no indication she'd caught on. "Let's get this over with."

I barked out a laugh, feeling the tension easing from my shoulders and guided her to the dining room. The others had already served themselves, so I pulled out Sadie's chair so she could sit. Before I sat down, I dished up a helping of chicken noodle casserole for her and silently thanked Doc for making something that would be easy on her stomach.

Throughout dinner, I noticed Sadie glancing around the table at everyone. I didn't think she realized how much her expressions revealed, and I didn't tell her. At first, her nervousness was evident, but she eventually began to relax. My family had that effect on people. None of us had ever met a stranger.

As I watched Sadie, I took in the conversations around me. Griffin and Aiden talked about dogs, and I noticed Sadie's eyes light up. Rather than join in the conversation, she held back. Doc discussed medical equipment with Nell, and it sounded like their list was going to be quite expensive.

After a while, all conversation halted, and all eyes were on Sadie.

"So, Red, how are you feeling?" Griffin asked around a big bite of food.

"I'm feeling okay. Tired. Sore."

Griffin snorted at her response. "Yeah, I bet. So, what can you tell us about what happened?" Griffin wasn't the best at small talk. He shrugged his shoulders as I mean mugged him.

"Can we finish eating first? It's not really great dinner conversation," Sadie replied.

"Of course. Griff here," Aiden pointed to Griffin with his

fork, "just likes to get to the point. He's our go-to guy for gathering intel, so he kind of jumps right into things. Ignore him."

Conversation turned back to mundane things while everyone finished eating. I helped Doc clear the table and when I sat back down, I heard Nell, Brie and Sadie talking about having a girls' night out at Dusty's.

"I'm not so sure that's a good idea," I interrupted them.

"And why the hell not?" Brie asked, clearly pissed.

"Because we don't know what we're dealing with yet and until we do, I don't want her unprotected."

"Jesus, ya big lug. Nell and I will be with her. What are we, chopped liver?"

"I didn't say that. I just don't—"

The shrillest whistle I'd ever heard pierced the air. Both Brie and I immediately shut up.

"That's better. Now, you can stop talking about me like I'm not here. I may have been through a lot and come across as a scared, spineless twit, but I'm not. At least, I haven't always been." Sadie turned and addressed Brie. "I appreciate you standing up for me, but I can talk for myself. And you," Sadie pivoted and pointed to me, "you need to tone it down a bit. I know you think you're protecting me, but being all sexy alpha isn't going to fly with me."

She just called me sexy. Yeah, I can work with that.

"Fine. You can go to Dusty's, but I don't have to like it."

"I'm so glad I have your permission. Not that it would have mattered either way. I'm going because I want to go whether you like it or not," Sadie said.

I was angry but she was right. I had no say so in what she did. I wanted her to be free and have fun, so why was I being such an asshole about it? And because I didn't like the answer to that question, I changed the subject.

"You're right. I'm sorry. Why don't we move on and talk about what happened the night I found you?"

"Okay. What do you want to know?" Sadie asked, stalling a little.

"Start wherever you feel most comfortable," I suggested.

"Okay. Well...okay. I guess I'll start at the beginning." She paused and took a deep breath. "Ian and I have been married for four years." Over the next few minutes, she explained how they'd met at Ian's family business when she was nineteen and then about her relationship with him up prior to the marriage. It didn't sound like a fairy-tale, but who was I to judge?

"Then there was the honeymoon and that is when everything changed. It happened slowly and I guess I didn't recognize the signs. We argued a lot, but never about anything important. I chalked it up to stress from work and the nuances of being newlyweds. Trying to learn each other's quirks and day-to-day habits. We didn't live together before getting married, so in my mind, that seemed like a logical explanation. Not really ever having an example of what a marriage should be, I guess I thought it was normal."

At some point during Sadie's speech I had moved closer to her. The others were hung up on her every word.

"We'd been married for two years before he hit me. The power had gone out earlier that day and dinner wasn't ready in time. He yelled at me for that and I was so pissed because it wasn't my fault. I yelled back and stormed to our bedroom and slammed the door. Ian followed me and I was so angry and hurt that I was intent on yelling at him some more. I didn't get the chance. He slapped me. I was stunned but he was so apologetic that I forgave him."

Tears were streaming down Sadie's face and I couldn't stop myself from reaching out to brush them away. She gave me a grateful smile before continuing.

"Looking back, I realize he was never really as perfect as I thought, but at the time I had latched onto anything resembling a family and allowed myself to ignore the signs of a bigger problem. He held himself in check for a few weeks, but the second slap came and then the third. It progressed from there."

My hands fisted at my sides as she talked about how she'd been beaten when she'd gotten pregnant and then miscarried as a result. Her facial expressions gave me the feeling that she was glossing over something, but I let it go.

"After that, Ian made me quit my job. He didn't want anyone to see my injuries. I wasn't allowed to leave the house or even have a cell phone. I had no friends. I was only allowed books. At first, he would only let me read what I already had at the house but I was…um…I was able to eventually…" Sadie looked down at her feet. She had stood up a while ago and began to pace as she talked, but now she stood still and looked uncertain. "I was able to *convince* him to start taking me to the library for more books. He would drop me off and pick me back up."

Sadie stopped talking and just stared at nothing. She had been crying at the beginning of her story, but now her eyes were dry. It was almost like she had detached and was talking about someone other than herself. I watched as she drew up her shoulders, straightened her spine and lifted her head. *He hasn't completely broken her.*

The rest of the story poured out of her. She explained how she'd worked at the library and opened a bank account. How she'd purchased a car and kept it hidden from him. How, after months of planning, she'd reached her breaking point.

"The night you found me…that was my getaway." Sadie looked me right in the eyes as she spoke. "Ian came home from work in a rage. As soon as he walked through the door all hell broke loose. He just started beating me. He punched me, kicked me…I knew he was going to kill me."

I stiffened at her words. What had that felt like? To know that your time was up and the person that was making it happen was the one person you should be able to trust.

"I managed to get to the car and just started driving. He followed me for a while, but I lost him around Columbus. I was so tired, but the adrenaline kept me going. When I saw the sign for Spiceland, it seemed like it would be as good a place as any, so I took the exit and was going to get a room for the night. Then," she shrugged, "light's out."

Holy fuck! I had been impressed with Sadie before, simply because she'd fought to live but now…now I was in awe of her. She'd clearly been through more than most women and she'd survived.

"Fuck. I'm sorry you went through all of that. I'm glad you were able to tell us, though. It'll make helping you a little easier. And we'll feel better about making that fucker pay," I said as I tried to rein in my anger.

"What're you gonna do?" Sadie asked this quietly. It was obvious that telling us what she did had taken a toll on her. She looked exhausted.

"Well, we're going to plan," Nell said. I was glad Nell spoke up because I certainly wouldn't have put it quite as nicely.

"Plan what?"

"Plan how to nail him for all the shit he's done to you," I growled.

"Oh. Okay. I can live with that. On one condition."

"What's your condition?" I asked.

"Don't leave me out of *any* of it. You," she looked around the table to take in everyone, "have to promise to keep me in the loop at all times. I had enough bullshit with Ian, and I won't be kept in the dark. This is non-negotiable for me."

"We can do that," Nell responded, a little too quickly. I didn't correct her because I did plan to keep Sadie informed about what was going on. However, I couldn't promise that I wouldn't *ever* keep something from her. I wanted to protect her, and I would do whatever was necessary to do that even if it meant a few secrets.

16

MICAH

The others had filed out of the dining room a few minutes ago after they each gave Sadie a hug. I couldn't tell how Sadie felt about those hugs, but she hadn't flinched so that was something. When we were alone, I could tell that her nerves were starting to get the better of her. I wanted to put her at ease, but I wasn't sure how. I didn't want to scare her.

"Sweetness, I'm not going to jump you or attack now that we're alone. Why don't we get you to bed? You look exhausted." I tried to keep my voice low and even. Despite my promise to myself that I would give her time and space, the way she had alternated between biting her bottom lip and sweeping her tongue out across it made my pants feel about five sizes too small.

"I am kinda tired," she said shyly. We couldn't have that.

"We don't have to stay here in the main house. We can go to my cabin if you want. It's on the property but it would give you a little more peace and quiet." I secretly hoped she'd agree to that. It wasn't like I'd been expecting sex, but I had wanted to get her alone.

She ducked her head for a minute, and I could see the faintest blush as it rose up her neck and up even farther onto her cheeks.

"Um, okay. Yeah, that would be nice."

"Are you sure? It's your call. I can sleep anywhere and I'm pretty sure you're tired enough to sleep wherever you lie down." I wanted, no *needed*, her to know she had choices. She would always have choices with me.

"I'm sure. Everyone has been really great here, but it would be nice to get out of this house and have a change of scenery. I never got enough of that before." Something flashed in her eyes when she said that, but I let it go.

"Okay. Let's go grab your pain meds from my room and then we'll go. I'll come back over and get your clothes and things in the morning."

"Whatever's easiest."

"I won't even make you get on Rhiannon tonight."

"Who's Rhiannon and why would I have to get on her?" I had tried to put her at ease with that comment, but I could see I hadn't succeeded.

"Rhiannon is my bike. I usually ride her, no pun intended, whenever I can but with your injuries, I don't want to take any chances jarring you or anything. We'll take the Jeep."

"Why do guys always do that?" She looked annoyed. Oh, hell.

"Do what, sweetness?"

"Give your *toys* female names. And it's always something sexy. I mean, *Rhiannon?* Come on." She rolled her eyes and even managed to make that sexy. I was so fucked.

"It would sound pretty ridiculous if I said I was going for a ride on Derek now, wouldn't it? Besides, anything I straddle is going to be female." And then it was time to change the subject. I shifted my legs a bit because my pants had become *six* sizes too small. "Ready?"

"Not for what you're thinking, but yes, I'm ready to go get my stuff. Well, just my pain meds for now, if you're sure."

"I'm sure." I slowly wrapped my arms around her. I hated the pain that had crossed her features as she spoke. It wasn't lost on me that she relaxed into my hold, and I realized that my imagination had nothing on the feel of her body pressed against mine.

~

Sadie

After Micah had slid his arms around me, all of my fear and anger and panic faded away until all that was left was the *heat*. The heat of his body. The heat that swirled in my gut. The heat between my legs. My nipples hardened, and I only allowed myself a second more before I stepped away.

That was about an hour ago and now we were at Micah's cabin. Micah had shown me around when we arrived, and I was in love. The kitchen was amazing, and I hoped I got to cook in it. Not that I'd ever been a good cook but there were a few dishes I could make.

Micah told me I could sleep in the spare room. It was so cozy in here. One wall was lined with bookshelves full of all different genres. There was a full bed with a colorful quilt I couldn't wait to curl up under. A nightstand stood beside the bed and there was a chair in the corner. The bathroom was between this bedroom and Micah's. I opened the door and peeked out to make sure he wasn't back from getting the rest of my things from the main house. Not that I didn't want to see him. I most definitely did. That was the problem.

As I tiptoed to the bathroom, I heard the rumble of *Rhiannon* indicating that Micah was back. Silently closing the door, I flipped the lock. It took me all of five minutes to brush my teeth with a toothbrush and toothpaste that Micah had left on the counter and use the restroom.

I unlocked the door, swung it open and ran right into the man I had been trying to avoid.

Micah's hands came up to steady me, because fuck he was a brick wall and I about fell down.

"Whoa. You okay?"

I nodded because words were beyond me at that moment. How did he do that? With just a look or a growled question he could make me *want* to do all the things I *hated* to do. At least I *used* to hate them. I was beginning to wonder, though.

"Good. Ready for bed?"

Again, I could only nod. My nipples were hard, and I started to feel flushed.

"Up here, sweetness." He put his knuckles under my chin to tilt it up. There was laughter in his voice. "Don't get me wrong, I'm glad you seem to like what you see but you looking at me like you want to eat me up is not helping the situation in my pants. I'm trying to be respectful here."

I stared into his eyes and didn't even realize I was nodding again. Micah tilted his head to the side, forever being patient with me, and I finally found my voice.

"Yes. I'm ready for bed." I tried to move around him but he stopped me with his words.

"If you need anything, I'm right down the hall from you. The door will be open. And Sadie, I do mean *anything.*"

17

MICAH

Sadie had been living with me for a month. There was no other way to describe it. She'd made her presence known and I wouldn't have it any other way. The many things she had accumulated on her shopping trips with Nell and Brie were scattered throughout the cabin and it felt so *right*. The more I was around her, the more I wanted more of her.

The first few days were a learning curve for me. I had never lived with a woman before. Never really wanted to. It took time to get used to her being there when I came home from the main house. The first full day she was here she had asked me about meals and which of us would cook. I could tell she wanted to cook, but I didn't want her to feel like she had to, so I told her that we could take turns. Let me tell you, I'd never eaten better than I did on the days that it was Sadie's turn. She made the most amazing pot roast and her Irish stew was to die for. She liked when I grilled steaks, and she gushed over my spaghetti. I learned that she was a picky eater but eager to try new foods, so we had done a lot of experimenting in the kitchen. Those were the nights I loved the most. Simply doing something that was so normal.

Unfortunately, those nights all ended and that had been the singularly most devastating part of living with her. When we went to bed, it was always in our separate rooms. I respected her enough that it would remain that way until she came to me. While my cock was equally as frustrated with the use of my hand as I was, that was not what was so devastating. Many nights I'd been woken up to the sounds of my woman (because she was my woman despite her not being divorced yet) crying or having a nightmare. Every time I heard her, I silently entered her room to watch over her. I wanted to wake her up and hold her, but I didn't. I didn't trust myself not to cross that line. So, I sat in the chair in the corner of her room and watched. Like some sort of creepy protector who wanted to take away her pain but also reveled in simply watching her exist. On the nights I did this she seemed to calm quicker than on the nights I didn't allow myself to get out of my bed. I told myself that her calming was because she could somehow sense me in the room and took comfort in that.

Crazy, right?

Sadie

The past month had been both amazing and completely nerve wracking. Micah had been so incredible with me. He didn't push me when I didn't want to talk, and he got me out of my head when I zoned out thinking about the past. The nights we spent cooking were so much fun that I almost forgot why I was here. We'd spent many evenings watching movies and relaxing. I hadn't relaxed in so long that I almost forgot how. But Micah was helping me relearn. And the flowers. Micah had brought home bouquets of forget-me-nots at least once a week since I've been here. At first, I would just find them in random places but when I finally asked him about it he shrugged and said they were the first thing he thought of when he saw my eyes and he wanted me to know that he was always thinking of me, no matter what he was doing or where he was. I mean, how sweet was that?

Then there were the nights I had nightmares. Micah thought I didn't know that he came in my room and watched over me, but I did. It was like there was an invisible cord that tugged at my heart when he came near, even in sleep. I wished he would curl up behind me in bed and quiet my fears by wrapping me up in his arms, but I didn't ask. Some might think that was because I was still married, but the second I ran, my marriage was over. No, my biggest concern was that Micah would get the wrong impression. I'd spent so much time with Ian using sex as a tool, a means to an end, that I was afraid that if I let Micah get too close, he'd somehow be able to tell. Like I had whore branded onto my body and if he touched me the brand would magically become a flashing neon tattoo. I wanted him to touch me, though. Sometimes I wanted it more than my next breath. I really needed to start being as brave as he gave me credit for and talk to him about it.

Jackson had been over several times, but it wasn't usually in any official capacity. Now he showed up again.

"Hi, Jackson," I greeted him. "Whatever put that look on your face can wait a few minutes. Micah's at the main house and if this has anything to do with *him* then I would prefer to wait for him to get back. Shouldn't be too much longer."

"That's fine, Sadie," he responded as he pulled out the kitchen chair, flipped it around and straddled it. "Got anything cold to drink? It's hotter than Hades out there."

"Sure. Beer, water, or tea?"

"I'm off the rest of the day, so beer please." He smiled as he spoke, but his eyes betrayed him. He was not happy about what he had to tell me.

As I put his beer in front of him, Micah walked in the front door and called out to let me know he was home.

"Sadie? You in the kitchen?" Micah's voice carried through the house.

"Yeah. Jackson's here, too," I yelled back, unnecessarily, as he walked through the doorway to the kitchen just then.

"Oh, hey Jackson." Micah shook Jackson's hand before he sat down. "Is this a business or pleasure visit?"

"I wish I could say pleasure, but it's business," Jackson answered before he directed his attention to me. "Why don't you sit down, Sadie?"

"Just spit it out, Jackson. I have plans to go out to Dusty's with the girls and the sooner we can get this shit over with the better. I need to get ready."

"Okay, here goes." Jackson took a deep breath. "Ian filed a missing person's report the other day. He's claiming that you're unstable and that you're in danger from yourself, the longer you're missing."

"What? Can he do that? Can he just say whatever he wants like that?" I dropped into the chair with a thud. I was not unstable, and I didn't understand how he could get away with lying like that.

"Unfortunately, he can. He's made it seem like you have a history of mental illness and he's worried about your well-being if you aren't found."

"I'm not in danger from myself. I'm in danger from him!" I shouted. This couldn't be happening.

"Sadie, we'll figure this out, but in the meantime, I think we need to revisit you filing for divorce." Micah interrupted.

"Micah's right, Sadie. If you don't get the ball rolling on

the divorce and Ian finds you in the meantime, he can claim all he wants that you're a danger to yourself. He's your husband, he's got more control. We don't want that. *You* don't want that."

"No, no I don't. Don't get me wrong, I don't want to be married to him anymore, but this is scary." I pushed my chair back, stood up and started to walk toward the door. "If you'll excuse me, I need to get ready."

"Sadie, maybe this isn't the best time to be going to Dusty's." Micah stopped me with his words.

"No, this is exactly the right time!" I whirled around, stomped back to Micah and jammed a finger at his chest. "I need this, Micah. I refuse to let him win. I am going to live my life and that means I'm going to go out with my friends and have fun. Besides, I'll be with Brie and Nell. Nothing bad is going to happen."

"Fine, but I'm going with you."

"The hell you are! I don't need a babysitter. And you have to go with Aiden and Griffin to meet that new client."

"I can go," Jackson interrupted. "I was planning on getting a drink later anyway."

"Jackson, that's very sweet of you, but no. I'll be fine. I'll have my phone on me and if I need anything that Nell and Brie can't handle, I'll call one of you. Please, let me have this one night?" I pleaded.

"Okay, sweetness. Have it your way." Micah sighed. "But you will call if you need anything?"

"Thank you!" I squealed as I threw my arms around Micah's neck and kissed his cheek.

"And I promise."

"Go get ready then. The girls will be waiting for you." Micah squeezed me back and swatted my ass as I left to get ready for my first girls' night out.

18

MICAH

*A*s I sat with Aiden and Griff at the diner, I thought back to the moment Sadie came out of her room, ready for a night with the girls. She had looked like sex on steroids in skintight jeans and a moss green tank top with a sheer lace back. I wasn't sure how she managed to keep her tits looking as perfect as they did because I hadn't seen any sign of a bra. And the black boots had made her legs look killer. I had been feeling better about her going out since Jackson had agreed to go to the bar, despite us having told Sadie we wouldn't watch over her, but after seeing that outfit, I was feeling tense.

"Micah," Griffin said as he smacked the back of my head. "Where are you, man?"

"What? Oh, I'm here. What were you saying?"

"We were talking about whether we want to take on Jason as a client. I think we need more info, but Aiden wants to move forward. It's your call, boss. What's it gonna be?"

"Well, I agree we need more info, but I don't think we should turn him down. His boyfriend clearly has a screw loose if the black eye is any indication. Call him tomorrow and invite him to the main house. We can go over specifics with him then and see if he can answer any more questions." Jason had contacted the BRB because he suspected that his boyfriend, Sam, had started using drugs. Jason claimed that Sam had recently become violent with him. Jason didn't want to leave Sam but wanted to help him if it was indeed drugs. That's where we would come in. The BRB would dig up some information, pay Sam a visit, and see if we could help.

I looked at my watch and saw that it was going on midnight. Sadie had been at Dusty's since nine o'clock and I hadn't heard from her. I tried to tell myself that was a good thing, but I was still worried. Just then my cell phone dinged with an incoming text. I glanced down and saw that it was from Jackson. Opening my phone to read the text, I was shocked to see a video of Sadie. She was running her hands through her hair as she danced on the bar, swaying her hips seductively. I could hear Luke Bryan's "Move" playing and Sadie was certainly obliging him. A text quickly followed the video.

Jackson: Think she's having fun?

Me: Too much!

"Fuck!" I said as I slammed my phone on the table after replying.

"What? Who was the text from?" Aiden asked, concerned.

"Jackson," I responded as I picked my phone up and hit play on the video for the guys to see.

"Damn," Aiden and Griffin said simultaneously.

I stood up, tossed some bills on the table to cover our tab and started for the door.

"Let's ride," I called over my shoulder. As I pushed

through the door and stalked toward Rhiannon, I heard Griffin snicker.

"This should be entertaining."

~

Sadie

Amazing. That's how I felt. I wasn't sure if it was the copious amounts of alcohol I'd consumed or if it was simply the fact that I was out with *friends.* I didn't really give a shit what the reason was, so long as the feeling didn't end.

"Shake it baby!" The drunk at the bar who had been ogling me all night wobbled on his feet as he yelled at me.

"Shut the fuck up, Joe," Nell yelled back.

Nell and Brie had immediately ordered a pitcher of Busch Lite when we arrived and while I wasn't crazy about it, we finished it off rather quickly. Fireball shots were next, and I hadn't stopped at just one. After shot three, my phone dinged with a text, and thinking it was Micah checking up on me, I downed shot four before I looked to see what he wanted.

Unknown: Hey babe. Having fun?

Me: A blast. Leave me alone Micah. I'm fine.

Unknown: Who's Micah?

That last text threw me, and I instantly regretted responding to the unknown number. Deciding to ignore the barrage of texts that came through after that, I turned my phone off, set it on the bar and downed shots five and six. I'd deal with it later.

"They're all staring at you." Brie shouted over the music.

"Who's staring at who?" I yelled back.

"Sadie," Nell gripped my shoulders to stop my movement, "take a look around. They're all staring at you. In case you haven't noticed...oh shit."

Nell's grip loosened and she spun me around to face the door. Anger flooded my system and I stomped toward the men walking into the bar.

"What the fuck are you doing here?" I poked Micah in the chest as the alcohol-fueled fury took over.

"I could ask you the same thing." He grabbed my finger and yanked me to his chest.

All my anger dissipated as I hit a wall of muscle. My hands braced against his pecs and I froze.

"Wha...what are you doing here, Micah?" I stammered as I tilted my head back to look up at his face. His height had never been intimidating, but coupled with the angry look on his face, it was now.

"You already asked me that, sweetness."

"I did?"

Micah chuckled rather than answer.

"What's so funny?" Narrowing my eyes at him I tried to get some of that anger back.

"You. So, how much have you had to drink?" Arms wrapped around my waist as he held me close and began to sway to the music.

"What are you doing?"

"Dancing with the sexiest woman in this place." His breath near my ear sent shivers through my body.

"Oh," I mumbled, allowing myself to relax and move with him.

"How much have you had to drink?" Micah whispered.

"A little."

"I'd say it was more than 'a little', if the video Jackson sent me is any indication." As if sensing his statement would set off my anger, Micah's arms tightened around me. I tried to push back from him but he held me immobile.

"Stop fighting me, honey. I'm not hurting you and you know it. As for Jackson, you didn't even know he was here so how can you be upset?"

I shoved myself away from him and he let me go. "Upset? I'm not upset. I'm pissed! I specifically asked both of you to let me have this night and you promised. How can I believe a word you say if you break your promises?"

"I didn't break a promise. I already told you that I would do whatever was necessary to keep you safe. That's what I did. Judging by the fact that you can barely stand upright, I'd say I made the right call," he boomed and that's when I realized he was right. I was swaying but it wasn't from the music or the dancing.

"I'm gonna be sick." Holding my hand over my mouth, my eyes darted around the bar to find a place to puke.

Micah scooped me up in his arms and carried me outside before setting me on my feet. I almost fell over, but his hands steadied me.

"Take a few deep breaths, sweetness. The fresh air might help," Micah encouraged, pushing my hair back from my face.

As I took the first deep breath, my stomach cramped and I dropped to my knees on the concrete, relieving my stomach of all its contents. Micah was behind me in an instant, holding my hair out of my face and rubbing circles over my back.

"Let it out, baby. You'll feel better."

The heaving stopped and I managed to rock back on my feet and rest within the circle of Micah's arms.

"I'm still mad at you," I said, pouting.

"Really? Even after I just held your hair while you puked?" Micah teased. "That wasn't pretty, you know."

"Ha, ha. Very funny," I croaked while trying to stand. I was beginning to feel a completely different sensation in my belly, and it was most definitely not from the Fireball.

Micah put his hand on my back as he guided me into Dusty's. Needing to get the awful taste out of my mouth, I excused myself to use the bathroom.

As I rinsed out the sour taste, Nell and Brie came in with huge grins on their faces. They crossed their arms and said nothing.

"What?" I demanded after spitting out the water I'd been swishing.

"So, you and Micah?" Brie questioned.

"No, not me and Micah." Looking at their faces, I realized they didn't believe me.

"Oh, please," Nell huffed. "We've been in this bar dozens of times and yes, he's danced with women before but never like *that*."

"Like what?"

"Like he was doing the bedroom tango standing up," Brie said, laughing.

Turning my back on them, I thought about what they had said. I'd felt a sizzle between Micah and me when we were dancing but then again, I always experienced skyrocketing temperatures when I was near him. *Did he feel it too?*

∽

Micah

"How long does it take to wash your mouth out anyway?"

Sadie had gone into the bathroom over ten minutes ago and I had to force myself not to follow.

"Uh, you did see Nell and Brie follow her, right?" Aiden joked. "They're gonna be a while."

"What's up with you and Red?" Griffin interrupted.

"What do you mean? Nothing is up."

"Oh, I don't know about that. I'd be willing to bet that a part of you is in a constant state of *up* around her."

"Shut the fuck up." They were acting like juvenile idiots, despite the fact that they were right.

Turning away from the guys, I caught sight of Sadie walking out of the bathroom. *Finally!* Even though I had recently watched her vomit, she still looked sexy as fuck. Unable to pull my eyes away from her allure, I ignored the continued ribbing from the guys.

"You ready to head home?" I asked Sadie as she sat down at the table.

"Nope. I'm not done yet." Smiling, she looked around the table. "Who's ready for a round of shots?"

"Um, Sadie, don't you think you've had enough?" I felt like a bastard for questioning her, but I'd hated watching her get sick.

"Maybe, but I'm not done yet, Micah. You've already broken a promise tonight. Don't ruin the rest of this for me." Her eyes pleaded with mine to understand and I caved.

"Fine. A round of shots, on me."

Cheers rang out and it seemed I'd made the right decision. Knowing that I had to drive Rhiannon home, I only allowed myself one shot. I spent the next hour adjusting the almost painful bulge in my pants as I watched Sadie down shot after shot and dance to whatever belted out of the jukebox.

As Dusty signaled last call, I stood and stalked to Sadie and pulled her close. She hadn't seen me coming so she let out a squeal before laughing when she realized it was me.

"Time to go, pretty girl."

"One more dance," she pleaded.

"Okay. One more."

Sadie spun away from me and headed toward the jukebox. Unable to take my eyes off the sway of her hips, I missed the switch to a slower song. Before I knew it, Sadie was back and curled into me, forcing me to move with her to the music. At that moment, I was thankful I'd broken my promise.

The song was over way too soon and before I knew it, we were all filing out of Dusty's. I held Sadie's hand to guide her toward Rhiannon. When we stood next to the bike, Sadie halted and tugged back on my hand.

"What?" I asked.

"Um...I can't...you don't..." Sadie was fucking adorable as she stammered. "I can't get on a damn *motorcycle.*" She had whispered motorcycle like it was a dirty word.

"Why not?"

"Because I'm drunk!" She threw her hands in the air. The action caused her to lose her balance, and I caught her before she fell on her ass.

"You'll be fine." I picked her up and deposited her on Rhiannon and climbed on in front of her. "Just hold on tight."

Sadie obliged and I had to fight the whole way home to stay on the road. Her thighs hugging mine and her hands pressed up against my abdomen was intoxicating. It didn't take long to get to my house, and I mourned the loss of her body after dismounting Rhiannon. As I helped Sadie off the bike, she got lost in a fit of giggles.

"What's so funny?"

"I'm smashed." The giggling continued until she had tears streaming down her face.

"That you are," I said, chuckling, before my emotions began to spiral out of control. I felt the humor leave me and my body tense.

"Why the serious face?" Sadie stopped giggling, crossed

her arms over her chest and poked her bottom lip out in a pout.

"No reason," I lied. "Let's go get you in bed. You're gonna regret all the alcohol in the morning." Turning on my heel, I started for the house. Like an asshole, I didn't bother to make sure she was following. Watching her giggle, like she didn't have a care in the world, had done something to me and I hadn't wanted her to see it.

As I stood on the porch and waited for her to climb the few steps up to my level, I used the breathing techniques I'd learned to calm myself. Sadie didn't deserve my frustration. I knew she wasn't ready for what I was feeling and that wasn't her fault.

"I'm so sleepy," she said around a big yawn.

"I know. Just a little bit farther and you'll be in bed."

"'Kay."

Once we were in Sadie's bedroom, I pulled the quilt and sheets down and turned around as I heard a thud on the floor. Sadie was hopping around and taking off her shoes. Once the shoes were off, she began to unbutton her jeans, and all of a sudden, there was a distinct lack of oxygen in the room. I knew I should tell her to stop and just climb into bed, but I couldn't move. Couldn't speak. Could barely breathe.

Sadie slid her jeans down her legs and stepped out of them before grabbing the bottom of her tank and pulling it up over her head. It felt like her every movement was in slow motion. I waited to see if she would remove any more of her clothes, torn between needing her to stop and desperately wanting her to continue. She stopped and the breath I hadn't known I'd been holding rushed out.

Once she was in bed, I pulled the covers over her and pressed a kiss to her forehead.

"Get some sleep, baby."

"Micah?" she murmured.

"Yeah?"

"Can you set my alarm on my phone? I'm gonna start looking for an attorney tomorrow," she said around another huge yawn. Some of her words were slurred.

"Sure. Where's your phone?"

"Dunno."

"I'll find it," I promised. "Now, get—" Sadie's soft snoring broke off the last of my words. I pressed another soft kiss on her forehead and went to find her phone.

Finding the device in her jeans, I smiled at the floral case she had picked out. After hitting the power button, I set the phone on the nightstand and went to my room to change. More comfortable in my boxer briefs, I returned to her room, picked up her phone and froze.

There were at least fifty texts from an unknown number, and I couldn't stop myself from reading them. It appeared that Sadie had thought the initial text was from me, but she'd been wrong. As I read the texts, my blood boiled because each one was more vulgar than the last.

Who's Micah?

Love watching your tits bounce while you dance.

Wanna feel my cock thrusting between those double D's?

I'm gonna wrap my hands around your throat as I fuck you.

Can't wait to watch the life drain out of you at my hands.

"Son of a fucking bitch!" I slammed the phone down on the nightstand and settled in for a long night of watching Sadie sleep while I fumed.

19

IAN

Sadie had thought she was so clever, but I found that stupid cunt and I was going to make her pay. It hadn't been too difficult to track her down. All I had to do was figure out the right questions to ask of the right people, and then it had been so easy. First, I learned about her bank account and then tracked down the purchase of her car. I also spent time digging into her history a little more and found out about her last foster home. Once I did that, I put the pieces together and tracked her down to that rinky-dink town in Indiana.

I had started to put my plan into action the night before, and I would have given almost anything to see the look on her face as she read my texts. When she mentioned Micah, it had thrown me off kilter for a second, but I recovered quickly. Thinking back on the things I'd said to her made my cock painfully hard. The images in my head that those texts evoked had me unbuttoning my chinos and grasping my dick and pumping it furiously. Not finding release, I began to take my imagination to another level. Picturing Sadie kneeling at my feet as I thrust my cock toward her throat and wrapped my hands around her neck brought me the explosion I craved.

As I stripped the rest of my clothes off and walked toward the shower, I thought about the protective order Sadie had served on me. Crazy bitch thought that would stop me but what she didn't know was that I had a connection to her new *friends.* Having to file a missing person's report was not what I had wanted but she forced my hand and for that she would be punished.

After I was dressed, my cell phone beeped. Thinking it was a text from my lover, I picked it up with a sense of anticipation. The release I'd found earlier hadn't satisfied me completely so a fuck later would be welcome.

I was surprised to see the beep was an alert to the tracking app that had installed on Sadie's phone as soon as she responded to that first text. Assured that it was untraceable, I was glad to see it was working. It was amazing what a person would help you do for the right price. The notification on my cell informed me that Sadie, or one of her goons, was trying to trace the number that the texts came from. They wouldn't find anything that would lead to me, so I wasn't worried. In fact, I was slightly turned on by the fact that she was trying so hard to find me. Or, someone was.

Not only would the app allow me to know exactly what was being done on that phone to find me, but it also established GPS monitoring so I would know where Sadie was at all times, as long as she had the phone turned on and with her. Since Sadie had never been allowed a phone while with me, I was counting on the fact that it was a novelty for her and she would not be without it.

I watched as several more alerts came across my screen It seemed that Sadie had become persistent in the time since she left. A quick flash of "What if?" went through my mind. There was no room in my plan for worry and second-guessing so I quickly pushed it away. Time to go and satisfy the beast.

20

SADIE

"Remind me again why I have to do this?" My head was spinning and I was pretty sure I was going to throw up.

Micah crouched down at eye level in front of my chair at the attorney's office. Mr. Groover's secretary had shown us in to wait for him to return from court.

"You don't *have* to do this, but you should. You know as well as I do that this is the only option if you want to be truly free." Micah's deep voice washed over me and my nerves began to settle. Having traded in his cut and jeans for a more sophisticated look, he was incredibly handsome, but it wasn't the look I was used to, and to be honest, preferred.

Micah and I had spent the two weeks following my drunken night going over and over the pros and cons of moving forward with the divorce. While I wanted to be divorced from Ian, I was reluctant to do anything to trigger his wrath.

"Has Griffin been able to find anything to go on with the texts?" I asked, already knowing the answer.

"No, which is why this is even more critical. You heard Griffin last night. It's like Ian's a ghost."

"He's not a fucking ghost." Shooting up from my chair, I instantly felt guilty for shouting at Micah. It wasn't his fault that Ian had somehow made himself seem like a figment of my imagination. If it weren't for the injuries I'd had the night Micah found me, I was fairly certain the BRB would have handed me over to the police to collect the reward Ian had promised for the safe return of his *crazy* wife. Strong hands settled on my shoulders and gently pressed me down in my chair.

"I know he's not, Sadie. And you know how I feel about your marriage. It wasn't one. This divorce is just a formality. But a necessary one."

"Hello, folks," Mr. Groover said as he walked into the office, and my nerves returned.

"Mr. Groover, it's nice to meet you." Micah shook the attorney's hand. "You came highly recommended by Sheriff Jackson. This is Sadie."

"Sadie, it's nice to meet you, even if it's under such circumstances." Mr. Groover had a kind smile but there was a shrewdness in his eyes that had me feeling like I'd made the right decision picking an attorney.

"You too." I shook his hand and quickly put my own back in my lap before he could see the shaking.

"Now, forgive me for jumping right in, but our conversations over the phone led me to believe that time is of the essence. Sadie, you've shared a little with me but if you don't mind, I'd like you to start from the beginning and tell me what exactly it is you need from me and why it's imperative for this divorce to take place quickly."

Glad that Mr. Groover didn't waste any time, I launched into my story. The process was grueling but an hour later I felt lighter than I had in a long time. Micah and the BRB had been great support and protection, but having someone on my side legally made me feel like I was actually going to progress in making my life my own. Before leaving the attorney's office, I had to sign what felt like a million papers and hand over a significant amount of money as a retainer.

While Mr. Groover listened to me talk, I occasionally caught glimpses of Micah clenching his hands into fists. The longer I talked, the more tense Micah became. As we drove to Micah's place, the tension seemed to get worse and I wasn't sure how to help him.

"Micah, what's wrong?" Unable to take the silence any longer, I turned in my seat as I spoke.

"Nothing." Micah's hands tensed on the steering wheel in what appeared to be an almost painful grip.

"Bullshit. You've been quietly fuming since we left the attorney's office. At first, I thought it was just having to listen to the shit that was my life, but now I'm not so sure. Talk to me," I pleaded.

"Leave it alone, Sadie."

I wanted to argue with him but something about his tone stopped me. It wasn't anger but something else. Something that sounded a lot like sadness or uncertainty. A completely foreign emotion to associate with Micah, even in the short amount of time I'd known him.

Micah

I felt like a bastard for not telling Sadie what was bothering me. She had just been through the ringer, *again*, and here I was acting like a child. But the anxiety that was welling up inside of me felt like it was about to bubble over, and I didn't want her to see that. All of my promises to keep her safe were starting to make me feel like a fraud. The warnings that the attorney gave kept playing over and over and over in my head.

Sometimes getting served with divorce papers causes the abuser to lash out or act irrationally.

In cases of extreme domestic violence, a divorce can trigger even more heinous attempts at abuse.

I think it would be wise to have someone with you whenever you go anywhere.

The warnings went on and on until the fear in Sadie's eyes was a palpable thing, and that made me feel helpless. It made me remember another time where there was fear in a person's eyes, and I'd ignored it. How was I supposed to keep my promises to her with all of the doubt coursing through my system? Needing to get my fucked-up emotions under control, I tried the deep breathing techniques that had worked so well for me in the past, and while they calmed me down a little, I still had that sensation of red-hot rage simmering beneath the surface.

As I parked in the driveway, I chanced a glance at Sadie and saw the hurt in her eyes at the fact that I had shut her out. I couldn't let her get out of the car without some sort of explanation, but I didn't know where to start.

"Sadie," I called as she was opening her door.

"Yeah?" Turning to me with an expectant look on her face, she was stunningly beautiful.

"Um, I know I've been quiet, but..." I wiped the sweat that had begun to trickle down my forehead and swallowed hard before continuing. "...I've just got a lot on my mind."

"Okay. Sure, that's fine. But Micah, I'm here if you need to talk. I know that I've done most of the talking, and you've been great, but I can be here for you even if I'm dealing with my own shit."

"Thanks, sweetness. I'll keep that in mind." Getting out of the car, I slammed the door harder than I intended to. I'd heard what she said, but I needed some space to clear my head. "I'm going to head over to the main house. I'll be back later." I turned and walked away.

When I got to the main house, I was grateful that no one seemed to be around. All was quiet, and that's what I needed right then. Walking in to the library, I was surprised to see Aiden. He was talking on his cell phone and hadn't heard me coming in. He gave a startled look when I stepped in front of him and quickly ended his call.

"Everything okay?" I asked.

"Sure." The look in his eyes betrayed his words but I wasn't in the mood to try to figure it out. "How'd it go at the attorney's office?"

"Fine."

"Bullshit," Aiden snapped.

"You know, you're the second person to say that to me in the last hour." I glared at him as I paced back and forth.

"Well, probably because it's obvious that something's going on in your head. I haven't seen you this tightly wound since our last—"

"Don't fucking say it! This isn't about that day. This isn't about me. This is about Sadie and how I can't fucking protect her!" Yelling at Aiden wasn't the answer but I had to get this rage out somehow and I didn't think he'd appreciate me beating his ass.

"And here's the third time...bullshit. This absolutely is about you. You've spent way too long blaming yourself for that mission and the clusterfuck it became. Sure, you've managed to lock that shit down for a while, but something about Sadie and the danger she's in has brought it all back. Have you even told her about what happened?"

"Of course I haven't fucking told her. In case you've missed it, she's got enough to deal with without me unloading my fucked-up self on her."

"I haven't missed it, asshole. How could any of us have missed it? We've all been in this with you from day one. Maybe not as deep as you, but we're in this together. And you wouldn't be acting like this unless that woman meant something to you. That being said, you need to tell her. You need to come clean with her. If anything is ever going to happen between the two of you, there can be no secrets. Quit being a fucking pussy and talk to her."

Aiden's head snapped back with the force of my blow and his hand flew to his nose to catch the blood.

"Jesus Christ, asshole! Feel better now?"

"Slightly." Running my fingers through my hair, I sighed. "Fuck, man, I'm sorry. I'm on the ragged edge here. Thanks for being my punching bag."

"Yeah, sure. Next time, give a guy a little warning though." Aiden laughed and I knew he wouldn't hold my lack of anger management against me. "Go talk to your girl. You'll feel better once you do."

Flipping Aiden off, I stalked out of the library, ignoring his chuckle as I went. He was right but fuck if I'd tell him that.

By the time I made it to my house, Sadie was in bed. I'd made a few stops on the way, putting off the inevitable. I'm sure a psychologist would have a field day with my actions, but I didn't give a shit. For the first time in a long time I was scared, and I had no idea how to handle it.

Not ready to go to bed, I grabbed a beer out of the fridge and plopped down on the couch. Flipping through the channels, I couldn't find anything to hold my attention. All my thoughts were on that last mission and how I was going to keep Sadie safe. Four beers later, I knew I had to try to get some sleep. As I walked to my room, I looked in on Sadie to reassure myself she was okay. She was sprawled out on the bed and looked incredibly peaceful. I gently closed the door, walked to my room and threw myself on the bed, not bothering to change my clothes.

21

MICAH

"Are you sure?" I ask Aryo for what feels like the hundredth time.

"Yes, I'm sure. He'll be there."

"Thanks, kid." I ruffle Aryo's hair as I turn to leave but his voice stops me.

"Play soccer later?" he asks in his broken English.

"Sure."

Leaving Aryo on the crowded street in Kandahar, I go looking for my team. Finding them at the rendezvous point, I fill them in on my meeting with Aryo and explain that the mission is a go.

Sweat poured off my body as I tossed and turned in bed. Knowing what was coming, I tried to pull myself from the grip of my nightmare, but I failed.

In position, my gut is churning. Something feels off.

"All clear on the north and west sides." Griffin's voice comes through the ear bud clearly.

"Copy. All clear on the south side. Give the word, Cap, and we're a go." Aiden's voice is rock steady.

As I'm about to give the all clear, something catches my eye.

Shit! Is that Aryo? What the fuck is he doing here? And why is our target yelling at him?

"No go! I repeat, no go!" *I stand up from my crouched position and break out into a run.* "Long range mission is off. We go in and handle this up close and personal." *I don't worry about anyone questioning me. I'm their leader for a reason.*

As I run, I get a visual on my team who are all running as fast as I am. We all know that we have to get there as quickly as possible in order to maintain some sort of control of this clusterfuck.

"You talked...stupid American...traitor to your country," the target yells at Aryo in Pashto. I understand a little of what he says, and it doesn't sound good.

"Target has Aryo!" I shout into my mic and pick up speed.

"Copy," the team responds in unison.

When I get close enough to see the fear on Aryo's face, I notice the knife in the target's hand.

"Aryo!" I scream, knowing that it's likely to completely fuck the mission. More than it's already fucked.

Aryo's eyes lift to mine and at that precise moment the target lifts the knife and slices it across Aryo's throat. As the life bleeds out of him, I throw my body at the target and tackle him to the ground. I hear my team as they take out the guards that came running after my scream. Zoning out, all my focus is on the target. Rolling around in the dirt, I wrap my hands around his neck, intent on draining the life out of him the way he drained the life out of Aryo.

"Micah!"

That voice is out of place in this hellhole.

"Micah! It's me," the voice sounds strained but insistent.

Bolting upright, I was still in Kandahar, squeezing with all my might, but the nails digging into my arm felt different.

Sadie's face was red, and she was trying to claw her way out of my hands when my mind finally started to clear.

"Sadie?" My voice was hoarse, as I scrambled back, horrified by what had just happened.

Sadie stood quickly. She was coughing and her hands were at her throat. She started to back away from me. There was fear in her eyes, and I'd put it there.

"Fuck! Sadie, I'm sorry. I'm so sorry. I didn't—" Sadie's hands came up to make me stop talking.

"Micah, I can't. I just...can't. I know you didn't mean to but—" She turned on her heal and ran out of the room.

Scrubbing my face with my hands, I sat for a few more minutes, trying to get my shaking under control. *I could have killed her.* Not able to stand being in the bed one second longer, I jumped up and headed for Rhiannon. I needed to clear my head before I could face Sadie and there was only one place to do that.

22

SADIE

Covering up the bruising on my neck was not as easy as I'd hoped. I'd managed to dull the purple and blue, but it was still terribly noticeable that *something* had happened, even if I still hadn't quite figured out what that something was.

I'd heard Micah yelling out in his sleep and when I rushed to his room and saw him thrashing around in his bed, I hadn't stopped to think of the consequences of my actions. Simply wanting to help, I'd reached out to him and tried to pull him from the obvious torture of his nightmare. I was rewarded by strong hands gripping my throat and a fear that had my head spinning.

Shaking my head at my thoughts, I picked up my cell phone for what felt like the millionth time to see if Micah had responded to any of my texts. He hadn't. I had heard Micah leave after I had rushed out of his room and he hadn't been back since. No responses to my texts. No return phone calls to my voicemails. Nothing. It was five o'clock in the evening and I was worried.

Having decided to go up to the main house to see if any of

the others were there, I tried to come up with an explanation for the bruising. I really didn't want to explain what had happened. First, it wasn't my place to tell the others about Micah's nightmare, and second...well, I didn't really know what to tell them.

"Hey, Red. What's up?" Griffin's voice cut through me as I walked into the kitchen.

"Griffin, have you seen Micah?" I had to make a conscious effort to not put my hands up to my neck to hide the damage. Judging by the look on Griffin's face when he finally looked at me, maybe I shouldn't have tried so hard.

"What the fuck happened?" Voice booming, Griffin stalked to me and grabbed a hold of my shoulders. "Was it Ian? Where's Micah?"

"Griffin, calm down. It wasn't Ian but..." I swallowed deeply before continuing. "It was Micah. But it's not what you think," I rushed to add and lowered my gaze to stare at the tiled floor.

"Shit!" Griffin tunneled his fingers through his hair, turned away from me, and began to pace.

"I don't even know—"

"It was a nightmare," Griffin interrupted.

"Um, yeah but...how did you know that?"

"Not too hard to figure out. Micah would never, and I do mean *never*, hurt you on purpose. And he's had horrible nightmares since our last mission. We all have them. Micah more than the rest of us, though. But we all thought he was doing so much better and hadn't had any in a long while. Certainly not since you've been here."

Taking in what Griffin was saying, I felt shame wash over me at the thought of my reaction to everything. If I had allowed myself to stop and think about everything, rather than let fear take the driver's seat, I would have remembered that Micah is the only person in so long that has made me feel safe. The only person who has made me feel anything really. And maybe that was the problem. I knew that Micah could hurt me worse than Ian ever did. He could break my heart and I didn't think I'd survive that like I could survive physical injuries.

Griffin's hand waving in front of my face forced me to refocus on the conversation.

"Where'd you go just then?"

"Um, nowhere. Just realized something." Not wanting to discuss what I had been thinking, I steered the conversation to the reason I had originally come to the main house. "Have you seen Micah? He took off after...well, after, and he's not answering my calls or texts. I'm getting a little worried."

"No need to worry. I know where he's at. Come on. I'll take you to him." Griffin started to head to the door and looked back as if to see if I was following. I picked up my feet and forced myself to walk. Glad that he was going to take me to Micah, another worry surfaced. What would I say when I saw him?

"Where are we going?" I asked Griffin as I mounted his bike behind him.

"There's this spot that Micah always goes to when he needs to clear his head. If he's not answering his phone and he's been gone since last night, I would bet my life that's where he's at. Just hang on, Red, and I'll get you to him." Griffin smiled as he talked, but there was still a little worry in his eyes.

Keeping my arms wrapped around Griffin as he sped down country roads, I realized that I didn't get the same spark or sense of awareness that I did when I rode with Micah. The drive was pleasant, and the Indiana scenery was beautiful, but there was no zing. After about ten minutes, Griffin eased the bike to a stop on the side of the road and pointed to a hill.

Sure enough, when I looked up, there was a lone figure sitting at the top. The hill wasn't so large that I couldn't make out who it was. Micah was sitting there with his knees drawn up and his arms wrapped around them. Rhiannon was parked near him, almost like he hadn't been able to part with her.

"Thanks, Griffin. I appreciate the ride." Getting off of his bike, I turned to stare at Micah.

"Do you want me to wait for you?" Griffin asked quietly while he remained on his bike.

"No, I'll be fine. I'll get him back to the house somehow. If I can't, I've got my cell and I can give you a call."

"Okay." Hesitation was plain in Griffin's voice. It was as if he was weighing his next words. "Ask him about this hill. He likes to tell the story and it may help him open up. If he's going to talk to anyone, it's going to be you. Good luck." Griffin chucked me under the chin and pulled away, leaving me to face Micah.

23

MICAH

Staring out across the fields, I heard the bike before I saw them. Sadie on the back of Griffin's bike. That sight twisted me up inside, but I mentally kicked myself because last night made it perfectly clear that I was too fucked up for Sadie. She needed tenderness and love and I was all jagged edges of something very broken. I tracked Sadie's movements as she got off the bike, talked to Griffin briefly, and then began her ascent up the hill. While I wanted to be alone, I knew that I had to give her some sort of explanation for what happened the previous night.

"Hey," she called as she got closer. The look on her face was guarded, as if she wasn't sure if she was welcome.

My mouth was dry as I responded, and I took a swig of the water I had left. Sadie stood there staring at me, and I tilted my head toward the ground, indicating for her to sit. She sat close to me, but not so close that we were touching. How I wished she would touch me, despite the fact that I didn't deserve it.

"It's pretty here." Making small talk wasn't exactly Sadie's specialty, but I appreciated the mundane topic.

"It is. I come here a lot when I need to clear my head."

"I can see why." Her deep breathing reached my ears. "So, all clear?"

"Not even a little."

"Wanna talk about it?"

"No."

"Fine. Then answer me this. Why here? What is it about this place that lets you clear your head?"

Now that was a topic I could talk about. Even if it was brought on at the suggestion of Griffin. He knows I love the story, so I suspected he told her to use it to break the ice with me.

"Safe topic. Smart girl." I chuckled a little to ease the tension between us. The tension I put there. "This is Elephant Hill. I love coming up here because I feel like I can see for miles. When I'm up here, everything else disappears and all I see is beauty."

"Why is it called Elephant Hill?"

"Well, the story goes that, back in the early 1900s, the circus came to town—"

"Seriously, the circus?" Incredulity was written all over her face as she interrupted.

"Do you want the story or not?" I didn't mean to snap at her, but I was still on the ragged edge and it just happened.

"Yes, of course. Sorry." The timidness was back and I mentally flinched when she ducked her head as she spoke.

"Well, there's two versions of the story. The first is that the circus came to town and on the last night, Tippo, one of the elephants got really sick. All the circus people tried to help but nothing worked. By the morning, the elephant had died. Back then, travel wasn't easy and certainly not with a dead elephant, so the town helped them find a wide-open spot and let them bury Tippo. This hill marks his grave." I chanced a look at her as I said that.

"That's sad, but things happen. What's the second version?"

"Well, it goes like this. Tippo was said to be the biggest, meanest son of a bitch. He went from one handler to another because no one could control him, and people always got hurt. It's said he once killed some men while crossing a river from New Jersey into Pennsylvania just because he didn't like them. No one was able to manage any power over him, not for lack of trying though. He was beat all the time in an effort for his handlers to gain any semblance of control. His last handler was part of the circus and when the circus came here, all of the animals were kept in an old industrial building on the other side of town. They were all chained to the walls so that they couldn't escape, or worse, do what animals do and follow their natural born instincts of predator and prey. Apparently, Tippo especially didn't like being chained up and he broke out of his chains. Several of the circus people, his handlers and some of the other animal handlers, all tried to get him under control but couldn't. They ended up killing him to stop him from doing the maximum amount of damage." I turned my head toward her and noted the tears falling down her cheeks before I continued. "Everyone in the circus, as well as the town, didn't want this to get out, so they all scrambled to bury Tippo's body. The circus is supposed to be a big family event, so it would have been bad press for them."

"That's, well, sad," she said, sniffling. As I watched the emotions that flitted over her face, I could only imagine the parallels she was drawing between herself and Tippo. Not being wanted, passed between people like they didn't matter, beaten, controlled, and eventually killed. Sadie may still be alive, but I'm sure a part of her died the night I saved her.

She still wasn't looking at me, so I reached over and gently grabbed her chin and turned her face toward mine.

The look in her eyes slayed me. Wrapping my arms around her, I pulled her into my lap. We sat that way for a few minutes, and I knew the time had come. I had to come clean about last night.

"Let me see." The request rumbled out of me.

Sadie knew exactly what I meant and swept her hair aside so I could see her neck. Breath left me when I saw the bruises. Bruises I had put there.

"Damn, Sadie." Reaching my hand toward the marks, I ignored her flinching. She settled quickly and allowed my fingers to graze her throat. "I...God, I'm so sorry. I never wanted you to see me like that, let alone be on the receiving end of my shit."

"I know. Micah, you have been nothing but amazing with me. I never thought you meant to hurt me. It just," she paused and sucked in some air, "it brought everything back in that split second. I'm sorry I ran, but I panicked. I'm sorry."

"Oh, sweetness. You have nothing, absolutely *nothing*, to be sorry for. You have to stop doing that. Apologizing for things that are not your fault or that you can't control." I hated that I was the reason she had doubts, and I had to fix that. "We're a pair, aren't we?"

I felt the tension in Sadie's body begin to disappear. The longer we talked, the more relaxed she became. But there was still something in her eyes. Something that triggered me to take the conversation a step over a line I swore I'd never cross.

"Can I tell you something, sweetness?"

"Micah, you can tell me anything. You have to know that. You know so much about me. Things I'm not crazy about you knowing. You've been there for me through my own hell. Let me be there for you."

I slid Sadie off of my lap and stood up. I couldn't let the ugliness of my sins touch her any more than they already had. I ignored the rejected look that crossed her face and began to pace. I knew I would just have to spit it out and I couldn't look at her while I did.

Breathe.

In.

Out.

In.

Out.

"My last mission with the Seals involved a boy, Aryo." I swallowed around the lump in my throat. I tried to even out my breathing and refused to let the panic take hold.

"Go on," Sadie urged quietly.

"We were in Kandahar. The whole team. We had a target that we were assigned to take out. A really bad man who had killed hundreds of people all because they didn't want to follow his beliefs. Other teams had tried to take him out, but they never succeeded. He would either outsmart them or kill them. Four different teams tried before we were brought in. We were the best of the best and knew we could do what had been impossible for the others. We'd been there for weeks and weren't having any luck when I managed to make friends with Aryo. He was just a boy, but we bonded over soccer. He loved to play and really, it was something fun in an otherwise hellish existence. After befriending him, I spent the next few weeks building a friendship with him. I knew I was there to do a job and I had never allowed myself to blur those lines before, but Aryo was different. He was smart and he had managed to make it to twelve without being sucked into the ugliness that surrounded him. I give his mother credit for that. Don't get me wrong, she did what she had to in order to survive but she also made sure that Aryo lived as normal a life as he could." I smiled as I remembered the woman who lost so much because of me. "Gabina, that was her name. You remind me a lot of her. Strong, smart, beautiful. Both of you are survivors."

"Anyway, I finally felt like I had enough intel to move forward with the mission. It was all planned out. Aryo let us know where the target would be that night and we planned to move forward. When we got there, something was off. I couldn't explain it then and I can't explain it now, but I *felt* it. Right here." I squeezed my eyes shut as I put my fist against my chest. "That didn't stop me, though. Should have. If I had listened to what I was feeling, Aryo would still be alive." Sadie gasped as I said that. That's when I turned away from her because I couldn't watch her as I finished. "The mission was a go, and everything checked out, on the surface. We had the target in sight but then I saw something that terrified me more than I can explain. Aryo was suddenly there. Who knows, maybe he had been there the whole time and I was just too focused to notice. Either way, he was there, and he wasn't supposed to be. I pulled my team back from the long-range mission and ordered that we move in."

The rest of the whole sordid story just flew out of me. I had no clue how long it took me to tell the story of the night that changed not only me, but the lives of so many others, but by the time I was done, my cheeks were wet, and my heart was spent. I realized that my back was still to Sadie when I was done, and suddenly, there was heat at my back. Sadie's body aligned with mine as her arms wrapped around me and her cheek pressed into my back. The fact that she hadn't run from me was astounding. How could anyone want to be near someone so evil, so broken?

24

SADIE

The pain that radiated off Micah while he spoke was like a physical disruption in the space between us. I let him talk and silently watched as the tears I'm sure he didn't realize were there fell. I even managed to sit still while he stood on the hill and looked out into the distance after he was done. But I couldn't sit still long. When I couldn't take it anymore, I stood and went to him. There was no thinking about it. There was no choice. I had to touch him. I had to let him know that he deserved to be touched. His body language had screamed that he didn't believe he was worthy, and that tore me up more than any mission he'd ever been a part of could. As my arms went around him, I felt his tears as they hit my arms and felt the shudders that wracked his body while he sobbed. I stayed silent. He needed this just as much as I needed to give it. Only when the shudders eased did I dare to speak.

"Micah, I am so sorry that you had to go through that. No one should ever have to feel the weight of that experience. But you have to know that Aryo's death is not your fault. You couldn't have predicted that outcome."

"But I should have!"

"How? Why?"

"Because...because if I had listened to my gut, Aryo would still be alive. Gabina would still have her son. My gut was the one thing, the *only* thing I could trust."

"That's not true. You also had your team. The team, I might add, that you have trusted my life with. Are you saying that they can't be trusted?" I heard the pleading in my voice, but I needed him to understand. He hadn't been alone then, and he was not alone now.

"Of course, I trust them. And yes, with your life. Hell, with my life. But I was in charge. It was my call to use Aryo for intel and it was my call that killed him."

"No, it wasn't. Think about it, Micah. Aryo trusted you, yes, and in a perfect world, everything would have gone down as planned. But Micah, that's not life. And we sure as shit don't live in a perfect world. You have to think about all of the lives that were saved because of that night. Yes, a young boy died, but how many more are alive now because of it? If Aryo were here right now, would he blame you? I doubt it. I bet, if he's truly like you described, that he would want you to focus on the good that came of that mission. Of his family member's lives that you saved. Of the thousands of children that can now grow up with a little more peace because of that night. And of all the people that your pain has driven you and your team, your family, to help. To save. That's what I think he would want for you. That's what I want for you. What everyone in the BRB wants for you. You just have to want it for yourself. And to allow those around you to help. You aren't alone in this. You never were, and I suspect you never will be."

Micah was still facing away from me and I could tell I was going to have to be the one to change that. He wasn't budging so I released my arms from his midsection and walked around to the front of him.

"Micah, look at me," I said as I reached up, put my hands on his cheeks and pulled his head down so he was staring into my eyes. "You couldn't have stopped it. If it hadn't been that night, it would have been another. If you really stop and think about it, you know that."

"Why are you still here?" There was no heat behind his words, only confusion, yearning.

"Because you need me," I took a deep break before continuing, "and because I need you just as much." I let go of his face and started to turn away. That admission was not easy for me, but I would have said almost anything if it meant it helped him through his pain. Before I completely turned, Micah grasped my arm and spun me back around.

"Say that again." He leaned his forehead against mine.

"I need you," I whispered.

Micah's lips crashed down on mine, and I was suddenly swept up in the hottest moment of my life. His hands wound in my hair, and I gripped his shirt like a lifeline. His tongue swept across my lips and I whimpered, which only urged him on. When his tongue darted past my lips, I lost control of my actions. My hands reached under his shirt, feeling smooth skin beneath my fingertips. His hands did the same and kneaded my breasts. The sweet ache of desire overpowered me and, in that moment, I wanted him more than I wanted my next breath. Micah had other ideas, though. When I whimpered again, he pulled back and stared into my eyes. The only sounds were the birds and our laborious breathing. I reached up and touched my swollen lips, and I silently berated myself for losing control. *What will he think of me now?*

"Don't," Micah commanded.

"Don't what?"

"Don't second guess what just happened."

"Okay, but—"

"No buts, Sadie." He cut me off. "It happened. It was incredible. You are incredible. And it will happen again. But not before you're ready. You said you needed me. Well guess what, sweetness, I need you too. More than I should, but there you have it" He tunneled his fingers through his own hair now, and I remembered what they felt like on my scalp. "Just don't regret it."

"I don't regret it Micah. I just don't want to give you the wrong impression. I know it's hard for men to stop." His gray eyes darkened at my words, but I pressed forward. "I never want to do that do you. But I could ne…never regret that kiss."

"Good. Now, let's go home." He grabbed my hand and tugged me toward Rhiannon. As he straddled the bike and I climbed on behind him, I wrapped my arms around his waist and hung on tight…and worried. *What have I done?*

25

SADIE

It'd been two months since I met with my attorney to begin divorce proceedings. Somehow, my attorney managed to get the hearing scheduled quickly. I was pretty sure it had something to do with the pictures that Micah had the forethought to take of my injuries and, for that, I was grateful. We were leaving in about an hour to make the trip. Micah and Jackson were coming with me since they could both attest to the shape I was in when I first arrived in Indiana. Jackson was due to arrive any minute.

"Sadie, everything is going to be okay. You'll see. This is a good thing," Micah said, breaking into my thoughts.

"I know. I just can't believe it's all happening so fast. I want this so much, but I've got a bad feeling. Like the other shoe is about to drop."

"Nothing bad is going to happen. Not with Jackson and I there. And your attorney was able to get the hearing moved to neutral ground so Ian doesn't know where you are and so you don't have to return to Pennsylvania until you're ready. It's all going to work out. And by the end of the day, you'll no longer be Mrs. McCord, but Sadie Harper." There was never any doubt that I would take my maiden name back and I was glad that Micah reminded me of the good that would come of this.

Micah's cell phone rang just as Jackson pulled up to the house.

"It's Aiden. Let me take this real quick and then we can go." Micah walked to his bedroom to take his call.

I let Jackson into the cabin, and he gave me a look full of sympathy.

"Don't do that. Don't look at me like I'm a victim. I'm done being a victim, and today, I get my life back."

"Yes, you do. And I'm proud of you, Sadie. You've come a long way." Jackson and I had gotten close over the past few months. He'd become like a big brother to me. We continued to talk about mundane things while we waited for Micah.

"Christ, don't kill me." I whirled around at the sound of Micah's deep voice.

"Okay. I won't. Now, do you care to tell me why I'm not killing you?" I asked.

"That was Aiden. Apparently, Scarlett's gone. She got a call from an unknown number and then just took off. He needs me to help find her. He knows what I'm doing today so he wouldn't have asked if it wasn't really important. There's no one else to help him. Griffin, Brie and Nell are out of town checking on a new case. Doc is with Emersyn. I'm so sorry sweetness, but I have to help him."

I took a deep breath before responding. "Okay. This is okay. I know you wouldn't back out on going with me if it wasn't an emergency. Jackson will be with me. I can do this. I can be strong and get through this." I was upset, sure, but it wasn't his fault. I couldn't rely on Micah for everything. And it wasn't like I didn't know what he did. He'd devoted his life to helping abuse victims and being one myself, how could I be angry with him? He'd left before on cases. I knew he hated to leave me but there was always someone with me, and Jackson would be this time. Besides, I'd be at a courthouse with other police officers around. Ian wouldn't be able to hurt me.

"Thank you for understanding. I know how important this is for you and I want to be there so badly, but I know that Jackson will keep you safe."

"Damn straight I will. I won't let that fuck hurt you," Jackson said.

Micah walked closer to me and pulled me to him. Hugging me he said into my hair, "You've got this, sweetness. Keep your chin up and make me proud." With that, he placed a kiss on my head, stepped back and turned to walk out the door.

I let him go and turned to Jackson. "Let's do this then."

Jackson drove the two hours to the courthouse and tried to keep me calm by talking about everything and anything under the sun. While I wasn't interested in conversation, he did manage to distract me enough that I was surprised when the courthouse came into view. I watched as he expertly navigated the parking garage across the street and found us a spot on the first level. After parking, I just sat there. I couldn't move. I heard Jackson talking to me, but I couldn't make out his words. My panic had settled in and I was losing focus on everything around me. Next thing I knew, a cell phone was being thrust at me and another voice was filling the car.

"Sadie. Sadie, do you hear me?" Micah's voice filtered into my brain.

"Ye...yes, I ca...can hear you. I can't do this Micah," I cried. "I can't go in there."

"Sadie, you can. You are so much stronger than you think. Think about how far you've come in the last few months.

You are ready for this. He can't hurt you there." Micah's voice was confident, yet soothing.

"But what if—"

"No what ifs, Sadie. You've got this! Now, go inside with Jackson and show this stupid fuck that he didn't break you," Micah demanded.

"He didn't break me. You're right. I'm not broken. Okay, Micah. Here I go." My panic had eased. Not completely, but enough that I wasn't frozen in place any longer.

"That's my girl," Micah praised.

"And Jackson," Micah's voice took on a steely quality, "you keep her safe."

"Count on it, my friend." Jackson took the phone from my hand and hit the end button.

"Thanks Jackson," I said as I leaned in and kissed his cheek. "I needed that."

"I know you did. That's why I called him. Now," he paused and looked down at his suit, "let's get this show on the road because the sooner we do, the sooner I can get out of this fucking get-up." Those words did exactly what they were intended to do. Made me laugh.

26

SADIE

$\mathcal{I}$'d been divorced for two weeks now. The hearing was over pretty quickly, and I managed to keep my composure. Ian couldn't explain the injuries I had and not only did the judge grant the divorce, he also reinforced the restraining order that had been in place. To my surprise, Ian's father had signed over half of the car dealership business to Ian several years ago. My attorney had managed to dig this information up and requested that half of Ian's money and assets be awarded to me. The judge agreed and, just like that, I became a very rich woman. Not that it changed anything.

Micah planned a weekend getaway to Pennsylvania to celebrate. We took the Jeep because, while I've ridden on Rhiannon with Micah around the property and into town, Micah thought that a longer trip might be a little much for me. I took him at his word. I loved riding on the back of his bike and being able to wrap my arms around him. I'd always held on a little tighter than necessary, but I couldn't help it. There was nothing quite so freeing as being on the bike, but the ache it created deep in my core was another matter altogether. And let's not forget the way Micah always managed to rest one of his hands on my thigh. Sometimes he'd just give it a little squeeze and others he'd rub his thumb in lazy circles. So. Fucking. Good.

Micah hadn't made a move since that one kiss up on Elephant Hill. Sure, there had been little touches here and there, but nothing like that day. Deep down, I knew he was waiting for me to make a move, but I was still scared. What if he wasn't making a move because he didn't think of me like that? I shuddered at the thought. Rejection from Micah would be awful. So, I didn't even try.

Packing for our trip, I was struck by how much Micah and his friends had done for me. As I went through the clothes that I'd bought over the last few months, I realized that I hadn't had this many choices in a long time. Ian hadn't liked me to dress up and what was the point? Work was the only place I ever went, so other than a few pairs of black dress pants and ugly button up blouses, I was always in sweats. That's what my wardrobe consisted of. Until Micah found me.

After throwing in my comfortable clothes, I put the black lace bra and barely-there panties, meant to drive Micah crazy, in the bottom of the suitcase with a smile on my face. I was so glad Brie had talked me into those. I knew I might lose my courage, or after confession time Micah might be completely disgusted by me, but a girl could dream, right? Jesus, we'd only had one kiss and I'd only been single for two weeks, but I was already imagining how I could seduce him to ease this ache that seemed to have taken up permanent residence between my legs. More often than not, I was walking around in wet panties and my fingers circling my clit were not nearly as good as I imagined his mouth would be when I was striving for release.

"I'm glad to see you're having fun," Micah's voice broke

into my thoughts and scared the shit out of me. I whirled around to face him.

"Holy shit, Micah!" I threw the baby-blue boy cut panties I was holding at him. Of course, he caught them easily and a sly smile formed on his face.

"Honey, I don't think these will fit me but I'm all for seeing them on you." He slowly walked toward me as he was talking, and I backed up a few steps until the back of my knees hit the bed. He reached around me and dropped the panties into the suitcase. I could feel the heat pouring off his body and when he stepped back, I immediately missed it.

"Yeah, well..." I wasn't sure how to respond to his statement.

"Well what, Sadie?"

"Nothing. Just...nothing." I couldn't possibly tell him what I was thinking just seconds before he showed up.

"If you say so. I'll move on to a safer topic, but first, know this. Those panties, and whatever else I'm imagining is in that suitcase of yours, are making me so fucking hard right now. I will see them on you and off you. In time." He crudely adjusted himself as he said this, so I knew he wasn't exaggerating. Maybe I wouldn't get rejected.

"Safer topic please," I whispered.

"Okay. I see by the way you jumped when I came in and by the volume of the music that you're enjoying your phone." I blinked a few times at the change in topic, because even though I asked for it I was still stuck on the fact that I turned him on.

"Oh. Yes, I am. I'll pay you back for that, by the way. And everything else." I wasn't crazy about having Ian's money, but until I figured out what to do with it, I could at least pay back those that had helped me.

Micah had come home one day, about two or three weeks after finding me, with a brand-new iPhone for me.

Before that, the only phone I'd ever had was a Nokia flip phone, and that was only until Ian took it from me. Micah had spent hours teaching me how to use the phone and how to download music, and it quickly became one of my favorite things. He had also helped me download the Kindle app so I could purchase and download books whenever I wanted. I hadn't done that often because I didn't have my own money. I had been too afraid to access my bank account for fear that Ian would track me down that way, but I didn't have to worry about that anymore. Micah had been so great about it and made sure that I had everything I wanted or needed. One night, I asked him how he could afford it and he explained that he had 'plenty of money' because he earned a lot while in the military and never really had anything to spend it on. He also explained that they received donations from numerous sources for the work that they did through the BRB, which he could access at any time. Hmmm, maybe I could give the money from the divorce to the BRB. I added that to the list of things to talk to Micah about.

"Is six o'clock too early for you to leave in the morning?" Micah asked, once again startling me because I was lost in thought.

"No, that's fine. I'm almost done packing. What're we doing for dinner tonight? Could we maybe go to the main house and ask everyone else to join us? It would be fun to spend time with them before we leave. Maybe Brie could invite Zach. It seems every time we set something up so I can meet him, something always comes up and he can't come." I knew I was rambling, but I couldn't seem to help it. Every once in a while, I reverted back to that timid woman, despite the strides I'd made and how desperately I didn't want to be her.

"Sounds like fun. I'll text everyone and make it happen."

Micah knew that he had to organize it because I still hadn't quite gotten the hang of group texts.

"Great. Give me ten minutes and I can be ready to go. We can head over early and cook for everyone."

"Works for me. I'm going to shower real quick, and I'll meet you in the living room in ten."

Well, damn. Now I was thinking about him naked.

27

MICAH

We'd been driving for an hour and I was starting to worry. Sadie had been leaning as far to her side of the Jeep as she could possibly get. She looked so sad as she stared out the window. There wasn't much to see, so I wasn't sure what she was looking at or looking for. This was such a change from last night. She had been so happy while we were at the main house with the others. She was disappointed that Zach couldn't make it, but I wasn't surprised that he wasn't there. He rarely came to Brie, she always went to him. But I thought that maybe Brie would be able to talk him into coming over to meet Sadie. Brie said that he'd been curious about the 'new woman'. I wasn't sure what that was all about, because he'd never shown any interest in what we did, but maybe I was wrong. I hoped, for Brie's sake that I was because the BRB and helping others was such a huge part of who she was that it was important that her significant other showed interest. Enough of that train of thought. This trip was about Sadie, not about me overthinking all of the things I couldn't control.

I reached over, put my hand on Sadie's shoulder and gave it a squeeze. "What's wrong honey? Why the long face?"

She no longer flinched when I touched her, but the look in her eyes at that question made me regret asking.

"Never mind. You don't have to answer that."

"No. I'll answer. I've been thinking about how to bring something up for what seems like forever and I think I just have to treat it like a Band-Aid and rip it off. Micah, there are some things I need to tell you, but I'm so scared you'll hate me when I do." She hung her head and I knew I needed to reassure her, but I was suddenly nervous.

Shit. This is it. She's going to tell me that she's ready to move on. Now that her divorce is final, she doesn't need me.

"Honey, no matter what you tell me, I could never hate you. Never. I need you to hear me and believe me when I say that. You are the most amazing, beautiful, brave woman I have ever met. Hands down. There's something here between us and we can't explore what that is until you completely open up to me and trust what I'm telling you. More importantly, you need to start trusting yourself. Ian is not here to hurt you anymore, and I'm not going anywhere."

"Don't say that. You don't know that. You *can't* know that. At least not yet. The things you don't know will change your mind."

I pulled into a rest area so we could talk because I knew this was a conversation I would want to give my full attention. After I parked, as far away from other cars as possible, I used the pad of my thumb to brush away the tears that were silently running down her face.

"Then tell me. Trust me enough to at least give me the chance to prove you wrong."

"I'm a whore." Fuck. Not what I was expecting.

"You're not, but why don't you explain it to me, so I know why you think you are?"

"Micah, I spent the majority of my marriage...no, that's not right because it was the furthest thing from a marriage as it could get...my time with Ian, doing anything and everything I could to get what I wanted. I used sex to be granted a few basic things like getting library books or getting a job or permission to watch television. Fuck and suck is what I thought of it as. I detested sex, but I used it. God, did I use it. Always as a means to an end. I prostituted myself to my *husband* so he would show me a little humanity and kindness. What kind of person does that? What kind of person has so little respect for themselves to do that? I'll tell you what kind. A whore." The tears were coming faster but so was the bitterness. If bitterness was something a person could physically touch, I was sure she'd be drowning in it right now.

"Sweetness, *no.* You are not a whore. You could never be a whore. You did what you felt you had to in order to survive." I reached over and pulled her out of her seat and onto my lap. She didn't put up a fight and instead curled into me and sobbed. I stroked her hair and rubbed her back. I didn't know how long we sat like that, but eventually she calmed down, so I continued talking.

"Sadie, look at me." I tipped her chin up until her forget-me-not blue eyes, swimming in tears, were staring right at me. "Listen to me. Are you listening?" She nodded. "The woman I am holding right now is still the most beautiful woman to me. We all have a past. It's not like I thought you were a virgin. I mean, you were married. Hell, I'm no saint. I've slept with plenty of women, but I know that none of them could hold a candle to you. I don't care about your past, other than the fact that it causes you an enormous amount of pain. With everything in me, I will make you see that. When we're together, because darlin' we'll be together, there will be nothing and no one between us. Not Ian. Not fear or pain. Nothing but you and me and the emotions I know we're both feeling." I took a deep breath because that was so much more than I intended to say.

"Oh, Micah. Please don't misunderstand. I want you. I think I've wanted you since the moment I could form a coherent thought after waking up. But what if I can't? I'm so afraid of what I feel for you. You make me feel safe and happy, but how do I know it's because it's real and not just because you saved me?"

"Sadie, Sadie, Sadie. It's real. You'll realize that, in time. And until you do, no pressure. But know that I am not going anywhere. I don't know how it happened but I'm falling for you. *Hard*. And when you're ready to explore what this is, I'll be here. Always."

I took a chance and leaned in. I had promised myself that she would have to make the first move after our one and only kiss, but I couldn't wait any longer. Her eyes widened before my lips met hers. The jolt of electricity that I felt made it difficult to keep the pressure light, but I wanted to let her take the lead from there. Slowly...so achingly slowly...she deepened the pressure and I felt her plump, silken lips part slightly. Despite my best intentions, that was all the invitation I needed to sweep my tongue into her mouth. Her arms wrapped around my neck and then worked their way up into my hair. It could have been two minutes or ten, but before I knew it, she pulled away. I opened my eyes and what I saw when I did leveled me. Lust. Pure, unfiltered lust.

"Micah, I want this. So fucking bad. But I need a little more time. Can we ease into it?"

She was afraid of my answer, but she was destined to be disappointed. Or not. Depended on how you looked at it.

"We can do that. But just so you know, that was the most spine-tingling kiss I've ever experienced. And I want more of that. Soon." Maybe that was the wrong thing to say but one thing I knew for sure was that I couldn't lie to her. Not after everything she'd been through and what she'd trusted me with.

~

Sadie

It'd been two hours since Micah had kissed me. Two agonizing hours of being so close to him without actually touching. I knew I had told him that I wanted to take it slow, but I wasn't sure I did. I couldn't keep letting Ian control my life and that's exactly what I was doing if I didn't at least see where things went with Micah. I knew it'd only been a few months since we'd met, but Micah was so different from Ian and let's face it, I took my time with Ian and that didn't exactly work out, so maybe I should just jump in with both feet with Micah. *You can do this. Be the courageous woman Micah believes you to be.*

With that in mind, I slowly turned my body toward Micah and studied him as he drove. I didn't want to distract him from driving, but I had to get this out before I lost my nerve.

"Micah?"

"What, sweetness?" He glanced at me quickly before he returned his attention back to the road.

"I've changed my mind." Talk about jumping in with both feet. I could tell he wasn't expecting that because he raised his eyebrows slightly.

"Changed your mind about what, exactly?"

"I don't want to take things slow. You're right. There is something between us. I'm not really sure what it is yet, but I am sure that I want to find out." I took a deep breath and held it while I waited to see how he responded to that.

"Sadie, you're killing me here. Can you be a little more

specific? I want to make sure we're on the same page, and I don't want to read anything into what you're saying that isn't there." I released my breath in an audible whoosh. Micah was *nothing* like Ian and this was one of the many ways that Micah proved it to me.

"Well, I guess what I'm trying to say is I don't want you to hold back anymore. I don't want to force things, namely sex, but I don't want to stop anything from happening naturally. Does that make sense?"

"Yes, it makes sense. And I'm on board one hundred percent as long as you understand that you hold all the control. We can go as far and as fast as you want, or we can go as slow as you want. I need to know that if you are ever uncomfortable with what is happening between us you will speak up and say so. If you can't do that then this won't work."

"So, if I'm in the middle of giving you some mind-blowing head and I change my mind you'd be okay with that?" I was testing him and I knew it, but I was only half kidding. Considering how the Jeep swerved a little maybe this wasn't the best time for testing or teasing.

"Christ, woman. You can't say things like that while I'm driving." While getting the car back under control, he adjusted himself as he seemed to have a habit of doing lately. "And yes, that's exactly what I'm saying."

"Okay. Just checking." I smiled at him and reached out my hand to grab his.

"You little minx."

28

MICAH

About twenty minutes from our destination, I realized I needed to wake Sadie up. She'd been sleeping for the last hour, and she looked so peaceful that I hated to wake her. Especially since I wasn't sure how she'd react when she saw exactly where we were. She knew we were going to Pennsylvania, but I kept the specifics of where we were going a secret. I knew I shouldn't have, but I had my reasons.

"Sadie, baby, it's time to wake up." I gently shook her shoulder. She had her head on a pillow on the center console and I'd kept my hand on some part of her body the whole time.

"Where are we?" She sat up and rubbed the sleep from her eyes. I knew once she actually looked around that she'd know exactly where we were.

"We're almost there. Did you have a good nap?"

"Any nap is good, Micah." She chuckled. As she looked around, I could tell the instant she recognized where we were. Her eyes grew round and I began to worry that I made a mistake not telling her.

"What the fuck? Why are we here?" She was angry and I hoped I could ease the fear I knew she was feeling.

"Sweetness, calm down. We're here because there's someone I want you to see. We're here because this used to be your home. We're here because you can't stay away forever. And we're here because I know you trust me to keep you safe."

"Who could you possibly want me to see? Micah, I ran from here. Just because the divorce is final doesn't mean that I'm safe. And this isn't my home anymore." She didn't sound angry so much as hurt. I hated that I hurt her, but I knew she'd forgive me. There was no other option in this scenario.

"You'll get answers to your questions soon enough. Trust me, okay? Please? Nobody knows you're here and I will never be away from you. It will be okay."

"I do trust you Micah, but damn, I wasn't expecting this. What if Ian sees me? What if he finds out I'm here?"

"He won't. We're only here for a few days and we won't be anywhere near his house. You'll be safe." I'd make sure of it. "Now, are you ready for your first surprise? This weekend is all about you, and I want you to try to enjoy it."

"As ready as I'll ever be." She looked around some more and a smile slowly started to form. This is what I was hoping for, what I wanted for her. "Micah? Oh my God, you're taking me to her, aren't you? I recognize this street. And these houses." She practically bounced in her excitement.

"Yep. That's where we're going." I pulled up in front of Gram's house, and as I parked the Jeep, Sadie started to open the door. "Sadie! Wait until I'm stopped. I don't want you getting hurt." I sounded like a controlling asshole, but Jesus, I didn't want her to hurt herself in her exuberance. Once the Jeep was turned off, she rushed to get her seatbelt off and practically jumped out of the vehicle.

When I looked toward the front door and noticed my

Gram coming down the walkway, I could only laugh and shake my head at the pair. Exactly what I had hoped for. I climbed out of the Jeep and walked around the back to get our bags. As I hefted them into my arms, I heard as the two women laughed and cried while they embraced each other. I was grateful to note that Sadie took care with Gram, who was getting older and frailer. Gram was doing the same, no doubt remembering the picture I had sent her of Sadie with her injuries. When I got closer to them, I noticed that Sadie's laughing had turned in to full-on sobs and I grew concerned. I dropped the bags and put my hands on her shoulders, quietly letting her know that I was there. Once my hands made contact, she released Gram, turned and buried her face in my chest.

"Sweetness, what's wrong? You were happy a second ago. Why the sad tears?" I asked as I rubbed circles over her back. Gram wore a puzzled expression and I gave an almost imperceptible shake of my head.

"I…I can't…Micah…why would…how could…how can she ever forgive me?" she wailed.

"Oh, child, there is nothing to forgive." Gram immediately interjected herself into the conversation. "You were a child. You were hurting. We all were. All that matters is you're here now. And you're safe." Somehow Gram had extricated Sadie from me, and she was grasping Sadie's head, forcing her to meet her eyes. It was hard to watch because I could see the tension in Sadie's body, but I knew that Gram was right and Sadie needed to hear it.

"I'm sorry. I'm so sorry," Sadie said, hiccupping.

"You have nothing to be sorry for, dear. Now," Gram lowered her hands, "let's get inside and catch up. These old bones can't stand out here much longer." With that pronouncement, she turned on her heel and walked up the sidewalk and into the house.

Sadie turned to me. I just smiled. "Come on, sweetness. We don't want to keep her waiting." I picked up the bags with my right hand, threw my left arm around Sadie's shoulders and guided her into the house. The first few steps she dragged her feet, but I could tell the moment she shored herself up. "Thatta girl. It's going to be a good weekend. Just relax."

Once we were inside, I left Sadie in the living room and deposited our bags in the two spare rooms. I didn't want to put our things in separate rooms, but figured it was for the best. At least while we were in my Gram's house. When I walked back into the living room, Sadie was standing at the fireplace, staring at all the pictures that lined the mantle. As I walked toward her, Gram stepped in front of me. I almost bowled her over, I was so focused on Sadie.

"Hi Gram," I said as I wrapped my arms around the woman who gave me a home and helped make me the man I am today.

"Hi, honey. It's so good to see you. And thank you for bringing my girl back to me." Gram's eyes were a little glassy as she spoke, but I could tell by her tone of voice that they were happy tears she tried not to shed.

"Anytime, Gram. And thank you for outside. She's doing so much better than she was when I first found her, but sometimes, she just loses herself in the past and can't get out without a little help." I kept my voice low so Sadie wouldn't overhear us talking.

"Of course she needs help. I can only imagine what that child has been through. Lord knows her life was no picnic before she came to live with us, but based on that picture you sent me, it just got worse after she left."

"Yeah. She's safe now, though. And I'll make sure she stays that way." Once again, I stared at Sadie, and my Gram's presence was fading because Sadie was fast becoming the only person in the room.

"I'm sure you will, dear. I'm sure you will," Gram said.

"What's that Gram?"

"Nothing honey," Gram chuckled. "Anybody want anything to drink? Coffee, water, iced tea?"

"No thanks," I responded and then, "Sadie, anything for you?"

"Mm, no, I'm good."

Gram went into the kitchen under the guise of getting a drink for herself, but she was a smart woman. I knew she was giving us a bit of space. I walked up behind Sadie and wrapped my arms around her and leaned my chin on her shoulder. She was staring at a picture of my Pap.

"I miss him," she breathed.

"I know. Me too," I said in her ear, as I slowly turned her around to face me. After staring into my eyes for a beat, she threw her arms around me and squeezed so tight.

"Thank you, Micah."

"You're welcome, sweetness. Anything for you."

Sadie stepped out of my embrace when Gram walked back in the room and went to sit on the couch. Gram sat down beside her, and I sat in the chair across the room. While it wasn't close enough to Sadie for my liking, I got to look at her that way, and that was never a bad thing.

"So, how are you feeling dear? You look much better than in the picture Micah sent."

Gram just jumped right in, and Sadie's head snapped my way.

Gram chuckled. "Well, shit, I seem to have stepped in it, haven't I?" The cuss word did the trick because Sadie's focus went from me to Gram before she busted up laughing. Gram turned to me and winked and all I could do was shake my head at the two.

"I'm sorry, I just…" Sadie snorted as she continued to laugh. "I've just never thought of you as someone who would swear. Not when you hated it so much when I would slip up when I lived here."

"Well, it did the trick. It got your mind off the anger and sadness and put a smile on your face. I'd say the little slip up was worth it."

"Okay, ladies," I cut in, "how about I take my two favorite girls out for dinner?"

"Micah, I don't want to go out to dinner. Please, can we stay in? I'll cook if you want." Sadie's request reminded me that going out was probably not the best idea, and I silently cursed myself for momentarily forgetting.

"Gram, does that work for you? We can cook and you can sit back and relax. We can visit and catch up."

"Sure, honey. That would be wonderful. Why don't you go unpack and get settled in? I'm not going anywhere. After you're both settled, we can do whatever you want." Gram was amazing. Always going with the flow. Maybe that's where I got my patience.

"Sounds good." I stood and waited for Sadie to stand. We then both went our separate ways. Her to her old room and me to mine.

29

BRIE

I was so unbelievably pissed. Zach was supposed to be here two hours ago. This wasn't the first time he'd been this late recently. I didn't know what was going on with him, but it must have been something big because he was normally more considerate than this. The guys and Nell weren't crazy about Zach and if I was honest with myself, I wasn't really sure I was anymore either.

After getting out of the military, I felt so lost. Then Micah tracked the whole team down and convinced us to move to Indiana. Only then did I start to feel like I could piece myself back together. The military was my saving grace at a time in my life when I needed it the most, and then we had that last mission. The mission that shattered us all.

Zach had brought me out of that dark place. It all started as a one-night stand because I couldn't have the one man I wanted, and it progressed from there. One night became two and then two turned into a weekend here and there. It worked out perfectly that he wasn't always home, because he was a means to an end. A way to forget *him*. It was getting a little old, though. Rather than being okay that I rarely saw

Zach, I got angry and I hated that I'd let him become that important. He didn't usually come to my place which meant I had to drive the forty-five minutes to see him. The sex used to be enough of a motivator for that drive, but now it's mediocre at best. I hope he can't tell that I'm usually faking it.

As I paced my living room floor and waited for him to arrive, I saw his headlights a few seconds before I heard the bass of his stereo. I'd asked him so many times to turn his music down when he picked me up, but he never listened. Watching him park, I opened the door so he could come in. He might not have been who I'd really wanted but he was so fucking easy on the eyes.

"Hey babe," he said as he walked in the door. He leaned in and kissed me. I kissed him back and he started to knead my breasts through my t-shirt. Sensing what he wanted and also needing some sort of release, I arched into his touch.

"Fuck, Zach. Let's go," I rasped as I reached for his hand and dragged him toward my bedroom. Maybe if I made it quick enough, he wouldn't be able to tell I was imagining another man.

As soon as we hit the bedroom, he tore off his clothes and I shed mine. Rough is how I wanted it and I wasn't shy about letting him know.

"Zach, fuck me. Fuck me hard and fast."

Gripping my hips, Zach spun me around and pinned me against the wall. I raised my hands above my head and braced myself. Thank God I was on birth control because Zach didn't put a condom on before thrusting his thick shaft into my dripping pussy. One hand gripped my hip while the other pulled my head back by my hair so he could suck on my neck. Whimpering, I slid my hand down and rubbed fast circles over my clit so I could reach release before he did. It wouldn't take him long. It never did when we were fucking like this. Feeling his body start to tense up, I increased my speed and pressure and before I knew it, I was moaning and coming harder than I thought possible.

Zach pulled out and I felt his arousal run down my leg. Smacking my ass as he stepped away, Zach said, "That's just want I needed after the day I had."

"Yeah? Me too. Be right back." Walking to the bathroom to get a washcloth to get cleaned up, I was struck with shame. I was still angry at Zach for being late and instead of telling him that like I'd planned, I had fucked him like a hussy the minute he was in the door.

"I'm gonna grab a beer. You want one?" Zach yelled from the bedroom.

"Sure. I could use one," I answered, as I stared at myself in the mirror. What I wanted was a good belt of the whiskey I kept stashed away.

Not wanting to end up back in the bedroom with him again, I quickly dressed and met him in the living room.

Wasting no time, I demanded, "Why were you so late? You could have at least called."

"Sorry babe. Got held up at work. My phone died, so I couldn't call." His answer sounded plausible, but there was something in his voice that I couldn't place.

"And what about last night? I really wanted you to meet Sadie, and you were supposed to come, but then all of a sudden you were 'too busy'." Gaining steam as I talked, I failed to notice him getting angry.

"I wanted to be here babe, but duty called. I had to tow two vehicles from the scene of an accident. What was I supposed to do, leave them there?"

"No. I guess not. I just don't get it. Every time we've had plans to get together so Sadie can meet you, you bail. She was really excited and now that she and Micah are out of town, it'll have to wait." I was getting whiny now. I hated whiny. Maybe I was just tired and should call it a night.

"What the hell, Brie? You know that my job isn't nine to five and things come up. This has never been a problem before. Why the fuck is it now?"

"Because now it's starting to piss me off. *You're* starting to piss me off. Just go home Zach. I can't deal with this tonight. I'm too tired."

He followed me as I walked away from him back to the bedroom. I tried to slam the door, but he flattened his hand on it to stop me.

"Go home Zach. We'll talk tomorrow. Maybe once I've had some sleep we can talk and make plans for everyone to get together another time."

He visibly tried to calm himself down. He knew I wouldn't take his shit. We didn't usually argue. There had never been a reason to. We scratched each other's itches and not much more. I knew what the others thought. They thought we were in a relationship and I'd do whatever was necessary for them to continue believing that, because the alternative was that they realized I was a slut who slept with one man while wanting him to be another.

30

SADIE

We were getting ready to head back to Indiana, and as I reflected on the weekend, I realized that I couldn't remember ever being so happy. Getting to see Sylvia again, reminiscing about the year I had been with them, and hearing stories about Micah's childhood had all been fun.

Brushing a tear from my cheek, I listened for Micah. He had gone out to the porch earlier to take a call from Griffin and asked me to pack the rest of our stuff. Suddenly, there were strong arms around me, and I relaxed into his hold.

"Why the tears, baby?"

"I'm so happy, Micah. You gave me something I never thought I could have back. You gave me my family," I cried.

"Aw, Sadie. You would have found your way eventually. I simply gave things a little nudge. Making you happy is one of my favorite things. Seeing you smile and laugh. Nothing beats it."

His hot breath in my ear made me crazy. Reaching deep within myself for courage, I turned in his arms and tipped my head back. Seeing the lust I felt mirrored in his eyes, I leaned forward and trailed light kisses over his chin, his cheek and finally landed on his lips. Micah did not disappoint. Deepening the kiss, he growled as he slowly backed me up to the bed and when I couldn't back up any further, he gave me a little push. Laughing, I bounced slightly until his body covered mine.

"We don't have time for what I want to do right now," he managed to say around tangling tongues.

"I know but I don't want to stop." I couldn't stop. Not yet.

Micah's hands cupped my cheeks and he slowed the kiss down until it was nothing but quick brushes of his lips on mine and I mourned the loss of that connection.

"How about this? I think we can extend our trip one more day. Let's drive for a bit and get a hotel somewhere? Just you and me. Sound fun?"

"Sounds like heaven. Let's do it."

~

Micah

The last couple of hours have been a true testament to my restraint. After Sadie kissed me, we took our time saying our goodbyes to Gram. I reassured them both that we could visit frequently and promised Gram I would bring her to the club so she could meet everyone. Then Sadie and I hopped in the Jeep and started driving. The conversation flowed easily while we drove, but once we were at the hotel some awkwardness filtered in.

"Sadie, if you aren't ready for this, we can leave. Just go the rest of the way home." Her eyes lit up at the word home.

"No, Micah. I don't want to go home. Not yet, anyway." She took a deep breath and continued, "That's how I think of your place, you know. Home."

"Good. I want you to think of it as home. I know it feels more like home with you there. I don't know what I'll do when you decide to leave." I didn't want to voice that last thought, give her any ideas, but I did anyway.

Sadie walked up to me and put her delicate hand on my cheek. "I don't want to go anywhere, Micah. I like that it feels like home. I wasn't complaining."

Putting my hand over hers, I brought it to my lips and kissed it. "Good. That's good. You can stay and call it home as long as you want."

Apparently, that was the right thing to say because Sadie pulled her hand from my grasp and wrapped it around my neck, pulling my mouth down to hers. Electrifying. That was my first thought when our tongues touched. My second thought was, I needed more. I let the kiss go on for a few minutes before pulling my mouth free and scooping Sadie up in my arms.

"Micah!" Sadie squealed. She was laughing, so I knew that squeal was a good thing.

Carrying Sadie to the bedroom of our suite, my heartbeat quickened, and I was afraid it was going to beat out of my chest.

"Put me down!" Just as she said that, I dropped her on the bed and watched her tits bounce on impact. My erection immediately grew painfully big.

I slowly leaned my body over hers, placing my hands next to her head, effectively boxing her in. There was a fleeting moment where I saw fear in her eyes, but it was quickly replaced by a hot look of lust.

"Kiss me," I demanded huskily.

With her hands running through my hair, she did. This kiss was different from the last one. There was just as much passion and heat, but there was something more. Something undefinable.

"I need you now, Micah. Please don't make me wait."

"Are you sure, Sadie? I need to hear you say the words. I need to hear you say you want this, want me." I didn't want to give her the opportunity to back out now, but I needed to know that she wanted this as much as I did.

"I want you, Micah. I need you. Only you. Now." That was all I needed to hear.

I gripped the bottom of Sadie's shirt, brought it up and over her head, taking care to trail my fingers over her belly, her breasts as I went. She responded with a shudder and her pupils dilated. With her shirt gone, I shifted my attention to her jeans. Her sinfully tight ass-hugging jeans. Carefully opening the snap and lowering her zipper, I looked up into her eyes and saw her watching me intently. I pulled her jeans off in a flash, taking her socks and shoes with them as I went.

Laying there in the skimpiest black lace bra and panties I had ever seen, Sadie was exquisite. I took a few seconds to simply stare at her and take it all in. She tried to cover herself up and I grabbed her hands, pinning them on the bed.

"Don't. Please don't cover yourself from me. My God, you're beautiful," I said, breathing heavily.

"I'm not. I'm...lumpy," she whispered.

"Lumpy? Oh, honey, you aren't lumpy. You're perfect. Every inch of you is all woman. Glorious, sinful woman." I knew she didn't see what I saw, but I'd work on that. By the time I was done with her, there would be no doubt in her mind that I loved every little thing about her. Imagined lumps and all.

"Micah?"

"Yeah, sweetness?

"Can we...can you...can we please just do this," she stammered.

"Oh, we're gonna do this, but I'm going to take my time. I want to enjoy all of you." As I was talking, I pulled Sadie so she was sitting up and reached around to unhook her bra. As her breasts spilled free, I tossed the bra over my shoulder. Sadie didn't try to cover herself again and I was grateful. Her nipples were a rosy pink and I watched as they hardened under my gaze. I give her a gentle shove so she laid back down, and turned my attention to her panties. Hooking my fingers in the band at her waist, I trailed them down her legs and was pleased by what I saw. She was a natural redhead.

I wanted to see all of her before I was so consumed with need that I couldn't stop, so I gently rolled her over so I could get a good look at her backside. Sadie squeaked and it quickly turned into a moan when I ran my hands up the back of her legs paying special attention to the backs of her thighs and stopping when I reached the globes of her ass. Such a perfectly sculpted ass.

"Perfect," I managed to get out. "I'm going to take my time with you, Sadie. By the time I'm done, you're going to be screaming my name." I didn't think I'd ever been this hard in my life, but I was determined to make this good for her. I didn't want there to be any room in her mind for anything but this, and definitely no regrets.

"Okay," she whispered.

I leaned over and placed my lips on her hip and traced lazy circles with my tongue, paying attention to how her body responded. She started to squirm, so I placed my hand on her back to still her. Once I was done with one hip, I trailed wet kisses across her lower back to her other hip, before turning her over and kissing her belly.

"Micah," she moaned.

"Say it again," I growled.

"Micah."

"Mmm. Get ready to scream it."

I took a second to scoot her farther up the bed so I could settle in and get comfortable. Once I had her where I wanted her, she had her feet planted on the bed and her knees bent and her thighs clenched tight.

"Can't have that," I said as I parted her knees and put them over my shoulders. In between her thighs I could smell her arousal and it was the single most intoxicating scent.

Without wasting any more time, I buried my face in her curls and flattened my tongue against her folds. While I was eating her, I reached up and started to knead her breasts and tweak her nipples, intensifying her pleasure. I didn't want to go too fast but keeping it slow and easy was almost impossible. Her juices coated my tongue and I swirled them around and up to her clit. Her moans were getting louder and her breathing was irregular. I slowly eased a finger into her pussy, continuing my attention on her clit. Her walls clamped down on that finger, and I knew she was getting close.

"More, Micah. I need more," she pleaded as she tugged on my hair. I felt the sweet burn from the sensation on my scalp, but damned if I was going to stop her.

Obliging her, I added a second finger, and crooked them both so I hit that sweet spot inside. Within seconds she shattered. She gripped my fingers so tightly that I was almost dizzy thinking about what it would feel like on my cock. Feeling her body start to relax, I eased my fingers from her and brought them to my lips. Looking her right in the eyes, I sucked them clean.

"That was incredible. Holy shit. I feel like I don't have any bones." Her skin was flushed and that flush deepened when she spoke.

Chuckling, I said "I'm glad you enjoyed it, but we're not done."

"Give me a minute to catch my breath," she said, laughing.

"No can do, sweetheart. I need to be inside of you. Now." I started to strip off my clothes.

"Not fair. I wanted to do that," she grumbled with the cutest pout on her lips.

"Next time darlin'."

"Promise?" she asked.

"I promise." She was staring at me like she was starving and once I was completely naked, I leaned over the bed to get a condom from my jeans. Her words stopped me in my tracks while I tore the foil packet open with my teeth.

"No condom."

"What?" I knew I couldn't have heard her right.

She started wringing her hands and I could tell she was nervous, but I needed her to explain.

"No condom. I um, got on the pill when you and Nell took me to the doctor. Having a second miscarriage, I just...well, I didn't want to take any chances. I was attracted to you even then and it seemed like the smart thing to do. I'm clean. I was checked out thoroughly the same day. So, yeah, no condom. I want to feel *you*. All of you," she rambled. I'd learned that she did that when she was nervous or scared.

"Are you sure, sweetness? I'm clean too and I would love nothing more than to be skin to skin with you, but I can use a condom. I don't mind."

"I'm sure. Now quit stalling and get inside me," she pleaded.

Chuckling, I took a few minutes to ensure she was still ready for me. There was no doubt she was still turned on. Her nipples were pebbled, and she was thrusting her hips toward mine trying to initiate contact. I reached down and ran my fingers through her slit to make sure she was still wet enough. I wanted to fuck her, not hurt her.

Satisfied with what I felt, I lined up my cock with her entrance. I slowly slid the tip in, and my body tensed. She was so tight and her spasming walls pulled me the rest of the way in. I was balls deep and I needed to take a second to gain some composure. Everything about this, about *her*, was so perfect I was afraid I'd blow too soon.

"Move, Micah. I need you to move," she groaned as she started to ease herself off me and set a rhythm.

Not wanting her to do all the work, I started to match her speed. I glided my cock in and out of her pussy and before I knew it the only sounds in the room other than our heavy breathing was the slapping of our sweaty bodies slamming into one another. I didn't want this to end but I could feel the tell-tale tingling start up my spine. Slowing the pace so she could explode with me, I reached between our bodies and put circling pressure on her clit with my thumb. That did it.

She threw her head back, dug her fingers into my skin and screamed my name. Seeing her in that moment of ecstasy and feeling her walls spasm and grip my cock sent me over the edge. Two more thrusts were all I managed before my balls drew up tight and that spine-tingling sensation erupted. Shouting her name, I felt all of my arousal spill into her.

Not wanting to hurt her, I wrapped her up in my arms and rolled over and pulled her tight to my side. This caused me to pull out of her, and I could feel the stickiness on my legs and her stomach. She rested her head on my shoulder, and rather than get up to get a washcloth to clean up the mess, I simply held her. She snuggled in deeper and I held her as her breathing began to even out and it was only a few minutes before I realized she was sleeping.

~

Sadie

I was having the most delicious dream. Micah's hands were running up and down my thighs as he licked and sucked on my most sensitive bundle of nerves. His mouth made the journey to my folds, and I immediately missed the contact on my clit. Needing release, I reached my hand down to flick my bean.

"That's it, baby. Make yourself come." Micah's voice broke through the fog of sleep.

My eyes flew open and I sat up so fast my head spun.

"Mornin' baby," Micah rumbled, still between my legs.

"Um, good morning. Micah, what are you doing?" I fell back on the bed because whatever he was doing, it felt so damn good.

"Nothing. Go back to sleep if you want." Like I could sleep now. The rumble of his voice only intensified the feeling.

It didn't take long before I was moaning his name. Once I was spent, I felt him crawl up my body and I opened my eyes just before he planted a kiss on my lips. I could taste myself on him and that turned me on all over again.

"Good morning," he mumbled against my lips.

"You said that already."

"Mmm, so I did." Ending the kiss, Micah rolled off me and pulled me to his side. "So, what do you want to do today?"

"I don't know. Don't we need to get home?"

"Yeah, we do, but we're only about three hours away. We can spend a little more time here. I paid for late check out, so there's no rush." He waggled his eyebrows at me while he said this.

"Can we now? And what would we do if we stayed a little longer?"

"I can think of a few things...or ten."

"I'm sure you can but my lady bits need a little break." We'd made love three more times last night after I had slept for an hour or so. Well, more like made love once and fucked like rabbits twice. While I was no virgin, I wasn't used to sexual marathons.

Laughing as he got up, he said "Okay, sweetness. How about we shower and get dressed and then order some breakfast? Are you hungry?"

"Starving," I said, and my stomach chose that moment to growl and grumble giving credence to my answer. Micah laughed at me, but I didn't care. He'd known me long enough to know I liked to eat and that was one thing I wasn't shy about.

After our showers, we ordered breakfast and sat in the main room of the suite and talked. Not about anything in particular, which was nice. I was kind of expecting things to get awkward between me and Micah once we crossed that line between friends and lovers, but if anything, things were easier. I may have told him earlier that my lady bits needed a break, and they did, but that didn't mean that I wasn't counting down the minutes until we could do it again. The connection I felt with Micah in the middle of all that passion was something I wanted again…and again and again. I'd never felt it before, not even in the beginning stages with Ian. As I thought that, my concerns about it being too soon after my divorce started to creep in.

"Sadie!" Micah's shout broke me out of my thoughts and my eyes snapped to his.

"Where were you just now? You looked like you were far away." Micah sounded concerned and I didn't want that.

"Oh, um, nowhere," I answered. "Wait, no. That's not true."

"Sadie, tell me what's on your mind," Micah pleaded with me. I could hear the worry in his voice getting stronger. "I don't want there to be any secrets between us."

"I don't want secrets either. And it's not a secret. I'm worried that my feelings for you are coming too fast. I mean,

I've only been divorced for two weeks and what will people think of me?"

Micah snorted and said, "Who cares what people think? I sure as hell don't. And as for you being divorced for only two weeks...honey, what you had was not a marriage. It was over the first time he dared to lay a hand on you. You know that. As for our feelings for each other, because it's not all one sided you know, that's between us and I don't think we should fight them. You said on the way here the other day that you were ready to take a chance and see where things went. Have you changed your mind about that? Because I haven't."

"Me either. Changed my mind, I mean. I want to see where this goes. I'm just…I'm still learning to trust myself so sometimes you might need to be patient with me is all."

"I can do that. Now come here," he said as he pulled me to him for a hug. Sighing as his arms encircled me, I felt myself begin to relax and the fears and worries started to slip away.

"Let's go home," I heard him say while my head was pressed to his chest.

"Home," I responded. I knew he meant his place, but it didn't matter. As long as I was with Micah, I was already home. And maybe someday, I'd be brave enough to tell him that.

31

MICAH

We'd been home for two days, and I had finally found the chance to meet with everyone to catch up on club business. Sadie had requested to come to the meeting, saying she wanted to talk to all of us about something. I had no idea what she was up to and I couldn't seem to refuse her anything, so here we all were in the library.

"Aiden, why don't you start and fill us in on Scarlett?" I looked at Aiden and he shifted in his seat.

"Well, there's not too much to tell. I still can't find her. She had her number changed or her phone shut off. Not sure which." Aiden and I hadn't been able to find her the day I missed Sadie's divorce hearing, and he'd put all his energy into finding her since then. "Griffin tried to use his *skills* to track her down, but no luck. I'm about ready to throw in the towel. We all know there are ways for people to hide and not be found if they want it bad enough. Hell, we've provided the means for many to do just that." Aiden ran his hands through his hair as he talked, and his frustration was palpable.

"Is there anything we can do to help," I asked him.

"Nah. I'm going to give it another week, and then I'm moving on. She knows where we are if she needs us."

"Okay. Keep me posted."

"Will do." Aiden finally stopped pacing and sat on the windowsill so someone else could take their turn with business.

"Griffin, how's your case going?" Griffin took on a young, maybe nineteen-year-old woman the week before who was trying to get away from her abusive drug dealing boyfriend.

"Pretty good. Nell and I paid the boyfriend a visit over the weekend. Fucking pussy. He was in the middle of a coke deal when we got there. He was selling to a kid who couldn't have been more than fifteen. We spelled everything out for him pretty clearly. He comes near the girl again and he knows he's gonna have to deal with us. Thought he was gonna shit his pants. After we left, we called Jackson and tipped him off about the drugs. Scumbag is now the newest resident of the county jail." Griff said this all with a shit-eating grin on his face. We didn't normally focus on anything other than abuse cases, but if something else came up, we didn't shy away from it either. Being able to take a drug dealer, especially one dealing to kids, off the streets was just icing on the cake.

"Glad it worked out. I'll touch base with Jackson and make sure he doesn't need anything else from us on that. I'm assuming you've got some surveillance we could provide if necessary?" We always did surveillance before going in and confronting someone. It kept us safe.

"I've got it stored. Let me know if he needs it and I'll transfer it to a disc for him."

"Okay. Good job. Both of you." I turned toward Nell and included her in that statement because I knew Griffin hadn't acted alone.

"Thanks boss," Nell replied.

"Moving on," I said, turning to Brie. "Brie, anything going on with you that we need filled in on?"

"No. Nothing. I've been keeping an eye on BRB property and making sure there are no security issues. I spoke with Jackson after Sadie's divorce was final." She turned to Sadie and shrugged her shoulders as if to say 'sorry'. "He told me that sometimes, after a divorce, one party becomes so enraged that they try to seek revenge. We agreed that with Ian's history of violence and his anger at her for getting a lot of his money, it wouldn't hurt to reinforce our security and make sure there were no holes in our system."

"Smart. Did you find anything?" Since I was standing next to where Sadie was sitting, I put my hands on her shoulders because I knew this was uncomfortable for her.

"Nothing that needed fixed. We did add some security cameras and you should all now have apps on your iPhones to access those cameras. That way, no matter where we are, we can be aware of what is going on here on the property. Sadie, you should have that app on your phone, too. Micah, we also added motion sensors to your cabin and if triggered, they will send an alarm to your phone. We figured your cabin, along with the main house, should be the most secure since those are the two places Sadie is likely to be. I hope that's okay."

"That's perfect. I don't want to take any chances. I really don't think Ian will try anything because that'd be pretty reckless on his part, but you never know. Better safe than sorry."

Griffin interrupted. "He might not, Micah, but I'm a little concerned. I wasn't able to dig anything up on him when I did my research. I mean nothing. If it weren't for Sadie telling us about him, I would think he didn't exist." Griffin winced as he said this. "And we all know it's not lack of skill on my part. I tried every trick I know, and I still couldn't find anything."

"I don't understand that either," Sadie spoke up. "I mean, it's not like Ian's a big techie or something. He wouldn't know how to hide like that. The only thing that makes sense is the fact that when he was made partner in the dealership, he came into a lot of money. I mean, the McCords don't just have that one car lot. They've got dealerships all over the country. Could he have hired someone to hide his online presence?" Sadie turned to Griffin as she asked that.

"It's possible. There are certainly people out there that are better than me at that sort of thing. No matter how he managed it, he did, so I don't think we can be too careful."

"Okay. All of this makes sense. Let's make sure we keep our eyes and ears open. Also, I want everyone carrying from now on, at least while on the property." I turned to Sadie and said, "That means you too."

"I don't like guns Micah." Sadie shook her head at me.

"Sweetness, I doubt you'll ever have to use one, but I want you to at least know how. I want you to have one on you, just in case. Most times, you pull a gun on someone and that'll stop them. You don't usually have to actually shoot."

"Fine," Sadie breathed. "You can teach me. Doesn't mean I'm gonna like it though."

"I know. I'm not asking you to like it. I'm asking you to just go with it and trust me."

"I said fine. Now, can we move on? Talking about Ian is giving me the heebie jeebies." She shuddered.

Everyone chuckled and I agreed to put her out of her misery. "Yeah, we can move on. Why don't you tell us why you wanted to be here today? I'm just as curious as everyone else." Her eyes lit up and she bounced in her chair. After a few bounces she stood up and turned to face everyone.

"Okay, so you all know that I came into some money recently," she began. She didn't need to reiterate that it was through her divorce. I knew she hated that the money came from Ian, so however she needed to explain was fine with me.

"We do," Brie said.

"So, I don't know exactly how much it is yet. I'm waiting to hear back from my accountant." She paused and took a breath. "Holy shit. I have an accountant. That just hit me. I have enough money that I need an accountant. Me. The woman who had to scrimp and save and scheme to buy a car and save her life." Sometimes she did this. Something would just hit her at the oddest times, and it was like she couldn't believe how it happened.

"Anyway," she continued. "I think it's somewhere in the millions, and to me, it's all dirty money. Oh, I know it's not, at least not in the typical way money is dirty, but it's dirty to me. It belonged to a man who made my life a living hell and I don't want it. Well, I didn't want it...until now."

"Why now?" Aiden asked.

"Because now I know what I want to do with it." She glanced around and took a second to make eye contact with every person in the room. "I want to give it to the BRB."

I had sat down in a chair while she was talking and was tipping it back, but when I heard those words the front legs dropped back to the floor with a thud. "What?" I asked.

"I want to give it to the BRB. Well, sort of. I love what you all do, and I want to be a part of it. If you'll let me." She hesitated so I stood up, walked over to her and tipped her chin up.

"Of course we'll let you. We want you here. *I* want you here. But I'm afraid I still don't understand."

"If you'd unhand her, maybe she could finish explaining, ya dumbass." Nell laughingly threw that insult out a little too easily, but I didn't care.

"Please, Micah. I'll explain. I promise. Just bear with me." Sadie's eyes pleaded with mine and I released her chin.

"Okay, sweetness. Please. Continue."

"Over the last few months, I've seen what you all do for others. For abuse victims. Hell, I'm the recipient of what you do. And it's made me realize a few things. First and foremost, I am so appreciative of what you've done for me. The safe haven you provided me. You all stepped up, no questions asked, to help a stranger, and there is nothing I could do or say to thank you for that."

"You don't need to thank us," I growled. I didn't help Sadie because it was the noble thing to do and I sure as shit didn't want her thinking that I was only in this because she was a case to me.

"Well, I thank you anyway. All of you," she swept her hand to indicate the room.

Everyone grumbled at the thank you because they all felt the same way I did. Sadie wasn't a case to any of us. She'd become a part of our family and none of us wanted her any other way.

"Second," Sadie continued, "I realized that I let go of my dreams a long time ago. I have always wanted to help people. I always wanted to go to college and earn a degree that would allow me to do that. It's time I chased *my* dreams and do what makes *me* happy. And third, what the BRB does is expensive. I don't know how you've all done it up until now, but I'd like to help."

I had stopped listening after I heard her say she was going to chase her dreams. The panic had set in. *She's going to leave.*

"Honey, I want you to chase your dreams, but…" I stopped because I didn't want her to see me as another barrier. Another man to stop her from reaching her potential. This might hurt me, but I'd live. If I took this away from her, she might not.

"Micah, just hear her out," Aiden said.

"Yeah, Micah, hear me out," Sadie jokingly said. "I think you're misunderstanding me. I'm not going anywhere. I don't want to leave. I want to stay here and chase my dreams here. With the BRB. I want to give a chunk of my money to the BRB so you have more funding to help more people, but I also want to build some more housing on the property so that clients…you need to start calling them that, by the way, and not victims…have their own space. So that you all can maintain your own space. And I want to be a part of each case. Working with the clients to help them emotionally. I've been where they're at. I can understand what they're going through in a way that none of you can." Sadie stopped talking and took a deep breath. No one spoke. We all just stared at her.

"Well," Sadie shyly said, brushing an errant curl behind her ear, "what do you think?"

"Sadie, are you sure? That's gonna take a lot of money. And you aren't obligated to stay here," Aiden said. I knew it pained him to say that. He didn't want her to leave either, but he knew she needed the choice.

"I've never been more sure of anything, Aiden," Sadie answered. "I've been thinking about what I want with my life for so long. I had nothing but time to think. Well, now it's time to act. I want this so bad I can taste it. But I also know it's not going to be easy, and I need all of you on board if this is going to work."

"Count me in."

"I'm game."

"Sounds like a plan."

Everyone started talking at once, but I tuned them all out. The only people in the library were Sadie and me.

I walked toward her, took her face in my hands, and kissed her. Before I knew it, there were cheers and claps from the others, so I ended the kiss and rested my forehead against hers.

"Sweetness, you are incredible. I can think of nothing better for you to do with that money. And the fact that you have so much faith in me, in my family, in the BRB. I'm speechless. Thank you."

"You're welcome."

"Now, what do you say we leave all these yahoos here and go to my place so I can thank you properly."

"I'd say 'Yes please.'"

32

SADIE

*T*omorrow was the big night. I'd been looking forward to our Labor Day cookout for a month now. Everyone was going to be there. Jackson had managed to take the night off and would leave the town in the capable hands of his deputies. Madoc was bringing Emersyn. Things were heating up between them, and it was so much fun to watch the big bad doctor fall all over himself when she was around. Brie had even been able to convince Zach to come, so I would finally get to meet him. Micah wasn't thrilled that Zach was going to be there, but he kept his mouth shut, for Brie's sake.

"What time does everything start tomorrow?" Micah asked me as we laid with our legs entwined after the most incredible wake-up sex.

"Around six. Jackson is working, and so is Emersyn. I think Brie also wanted to wait for Zach to get off work, so we didn't want anything to get going too much before everyone could get here." I ran my hand up and down Micah's chest. Even after having an orgasm not five minutes ago, I was still horny. He had that effect on me.

"Are you excited?" His breathing was getting choppy as I trailed my fingers down his stomach and gripped his cock.

"Mmm," I breathed. "Micah?"

"Yeah, sweetness."

"Stop talking." With that, I replaced my hand with my mouth and sucked on the tip. I could taste his saltiness and I started taking him deeper, letting my lips glide down the length of him. I felt Micah's hands grip my hair and he started to slowly fuck my mouth. Unfortunately, I had a strong gag reflex, so Micah was always careful. I felt him bump the back of my throat and he pulled himself slightly back, knowing that was all I could handle. He didn't mind, though. I made up for the lack of length I could take with strokes of my tongue and gripping with my lips.

Within minutes, his hands gripped my hair tighter, and I knew he was about to come. I curled my hands around his balls and before I knew it, he was shooting his hot arousal in my mouth. When he was done, I crawled up his body and swallowed every last drop.

Placing a lingering kiss on Micah's lips, I said, "Now you can talk."

"Thanks for the permission," Micah joked.

"Any time, hot stuff."

"Hot stuff?" Micah's eyebrows raised in question.

"Yeah. I was trying it out. It didn't work. Let it go." I laughed as I swatted his chest.

I loved that Micah had brought me out of my shell. He was so much fun to be around, and he made me happy. Every day with him was an adventure. He taught me how to handle a gun about a week after that meeting in the library. I still didn't like it, but I could aim and shoot, so that was something. We'd settled into a routine and I couldn't imagine anything different. I didn't know exactly when it happened or how it happened, but I was in love with him. I knew I needed to tell him, and I would. But I needed to know that he felt the same. Putting my heart out there like that was still scary and if he didn't feel the same way, I didn't think I would survive the heartbreak. So, I'd keep that little gem to myself for a little longer.

"What's on the agenda today, sweetness?" Micah intruded my thoughts.

"Well, we've got the contractors coming at eleven to go over the final plans for the new housing units. Then at one, we meet with my accountant and attorney to finalize the transfer of funds to the BRB. After that, not much. Just finishing up getting ready for the party tomorrow."

"Are you still sure you want to do all of this? I want you to use some of the money for you. You deserve it."

"Micah, I'm so sure. And this *is* for me. I'm still struggling with the fact that the money came from Ian, and this helps me reconcile that fact. Plus, it's going to result in a whole lot of good. Damn, Micah, some good really needs to come from that nightmare otherwise it was just…" I trailed off because it was still hard to talk about, even though I knew Micah didn't and wouldn't judge me.

"I know sweetness. I just want you to be sure. And if you say you are, then I'm with you, one hundred percent." His lips touched mine and we indulged in a long, lingering kiss before he pulled away and smiled at me. "We better get out of this bed then and get moving. We don't want to be late."

Glancing at the clock on the nightstand, I grinned. "I think we've got enough time for a shower…with a happy ending," I said, wiggling my eyebrows at him.

"You're gonna be the death of me woman," he joked. He swatted my ass and added, "Let's go."

After a pretty lengthy shower, I dressed in a pale-yellow pantsuit that I had bought so I could look a little more professional for some of the meetings that all this money seemed to require. While I was putting on the last of my makeup, Micah came in the bathroom and stopped in his tracks. He stared at me so intently that my nerves kicked in.

"What?" I asked him, picking at my clothes, wondering if I had overdone it.

He shook his head and stalked toward me. I backed up slightly and instantly regretted the action when I saw the hurt that crept into his eyes.

"Sorry," I mumbled as I stared at the floor. The next thing I knew, I was being picked up and deposited on the bathroom counter as Micah settled between my legs.

"Don't be sorry. Never be sorry for a reaction that you can't help." Micah's eyes bore into mine as he spoke, the gray swirling with so many emotions. "Eventually, the reaction won't happen and I'm here whether it does or not."

"Okay. Thanks," I responded with a little more confidence than I had felt a second ago.

"Is everything okay? You looked like something was wrong when you came in."

"Of course, something is wrong! How the hell am I supposed to sit through meetings with accountants and contractors when you look like fucking cotton candy that I just want to lick? I'm going to have to change because these pants are too damn tight now!" And with that proclamation, he lifted me off the counter and set me on my feet, turned and stalked out of the bathroom.

33

MICAH

The meetings had gone well yesterday, and I had managed to not make a fool of myself, despite the mental images running through my head the entire time. It was decided that we would officially break ground on the new cabins within the next month, and Sadie was over the moon about it. She had talked non-stop last night about the plans and I loved every second because it meant she was happy.

We went to bed and made love, and I held her all night long. I hadn't gotten much sleep, but that hadn't stopped Sadie from putting me to work this morning to get ready for the party. My latest errand: pick up the kegs in the next town over. I hadn't wanted to go that far but every liquor store had sold out because of the holiday. I wasn't happy about having to be away from Sadie, but everyone else would be arriving soon and Jackson was on his way, so she'd be safe.

I couldn't bear it if anything happened to her. *Nothing is going to happen.* I kept telling myself that, but the clenching in my gut told me different. The last time I ignored my gut, a kid died, so I hit the Bluetooth button and put a call in to Jackson.

"Yo," he answered on the third ring.

"It's Micah. Where are you?"

"I got caught up at the station, but I'll be leaving in about an hour. Why? What's up?"

"Nothing that I know of. I've just got this feeling. I can't explain it. I'm sure everything's fine, but I'm worried." I couldn't explain my unease, so I didn't even try. Jackson got it.

"Say no more. I'll wrap things up as quickly as I can and be on my way." He paused before continuing. "And Micah? Chill. Sadie's fine. Ian hasn't shown his face or made any trouble, so there's nothing to indicate he's going to start now. Your woman is fine."

"I hope you're right, Jackson," I said, running my fingers through my hair. "But what if it's not?"

"It is. You're just on edge. Call the house and check in with her. That should ease your mind a little."

"Yeah. Yeah, I'll do that. Just get there as quick as you can."

"Will do. See ya soon." Jackson ended his side of the call.

I speed-dialed Sadie's number, murmuring the digits as I heard the notes that indicated it was dialing. I had memorized the number the day I'd bought her the cell phone, even as I was punching it into the memory of my phone. It rang six times before it went to voicemail. I didn't bother leaving a message, but I did shoot off a quick text.

Me: Call me when you see this. Need to hear your voice.

I left it at that. I didn't want to worry her. Having assured myself that the text went through, I pressed on the gas pedal a little harder and tried to get this trip to town over with.

Sadie

Standing in the kitchen of the main house, I silently chastised myself for leaving my phone at Micah's cabin. I had been in a hurry to get over here to make a start on getting everything ready before the guests arrived and had left it on the nightstand. Maybe if Micah hadn't woken me up like he did, I blushed, remembering, I wouldn't have forgotten my phone. Oh well. I'd rather have that wake-up call than my phone any day.

Quit daydreaming and get to work. I listened to my inner voice and started to pull everything out of the fridge that I needed to make the punch. We were going to have kegs, but I wanted to make a spiked punch that would be perfect in this sweltering weather. While Micah was in town, Aiden and Griffin were working on wrapping up last minute details on their cases to ensure that they wouldn't be needed tonight. Nell hadn't made it to the main house yet, which told me she had had fun on her date last night. Brie had gone to meet Zach at her place and they would arrive together. They should be here any minute. I was so glad she had managed to convince him to come. I was excited to finally meet him. I'd heard so much about him, not all of it good, so I kind of wanted to see for myself what the big deal was.

As I leaned back into the fridge for the last of the ingredients, I heard the front door as it opened.

"Oh, hi Brie. I'm in the kitchen," I called to her as I closed the door to the fridge with my foot and dropped everything onto the counter.

I dashed to the living room to greet them and stopped dead in my tracks when I reached the doorway. I could feel all the color drain from my face, and I was too stunned to speak.

34

SADIE

"Hey, Sadie. This is Zach," Brie said indicating the man next to her. The man I had called husband for too many years.

"Hi, Sadie," Ian sneered sinisterly.

Brie finally registered the shock on my face. "Sadie, what's…"

"How could you, Brie?" I managed to croak.

"What are you talking about? How could I what?"

"That's Ian!" I practically screamed at her, pointing at him. "You had pictures of him! Micah sent you pictures."

"What pictures? This is—"

"Shut up!" Ian pistol whipped Brie on the side of her head, and I screamed. *How had I missed that he had a gun?* "Dumb bitch doesn't even know when someone is messing with her phone. And she calls herself a Navy Seal," he tsked.

"Bastard!" I yelled.

"Sadie, Sadie, Sadie. Is that any way to greet your husband? Come here and give me a kiss." Ian stalked toward me with his arms out, as if asking for a hug.

"Ex-husband," I spat at him. "We're divorced. Or have you forgotten that?"

"How could I forget?" Spittle flew out of his mouth as he yelled at me. "Every time I go to use my credit card, I'm reminded of that fact. I can't even take my girlfriend out on a proper date because of you." If he thought he was going to get sympathy from me, he was sadly mistaken. "You just had to go for my money? I could have forgiven you for running because, let's face it, that ship between us had sailed. But my money? I can't let that go."

I backed up as he continued his pursuit. "What do you want, Ian? Money? Will that get you to go away?"

"It may have a few weeks ago, but now I think I want to have a little fun," he taunted, and his voice was so devoid of emotion that the hairs on my arms stood up. "I was perfectly happy with my life. I had a wife that made my father happy and looked good to everyone on the outside looking in, and I had Brie. You tried to satisfy me, I suppose, but Brie made me feel like a man."

"How long, Ian? How long were you married to me and sleeping with her?" I didn't really care, but I needed to keep him distracted. Surely someone would be here soon.

How long has Micah been gone? Will he be back in time to save me...again?

"Does it really matter how long? Because you sure didn't wait to fuck biker boy. I hope you had fun, Sadie, because it ends now."

"You're right. This ends now. You don't get to control my life anymore. And you sure as hell don't get to tell me who I can fuck. You lost that right the first time you hit me." *That's it, Sadie. Be brave. Make Micah proud. You may not beat Ian at his sick game, but you can make Micah proud. Or die trying.*

"Bitch!" Ian roared as he lunged at me. He managed to grab a handful of my hair, and my scalp burned as he pulled me off my feet. Reaching up to grab his wrists to ease some of the pressure, I tried to think of what my options were. I could try to fight him and probably end up with more injuries for my trouble. I could give in and let him think he'd won. At least until I could come up with a better plan. *Fuck that!*

I went limp for a second, and Ian loosened his grip slightly. I took that moment to rear up, trying to catch him on the chin with my head. The moment I connected, pain shot through my skull and Ian roared. That gave me the second I needed to scramble away. Knowing I probably wouldn't get far didn't matter. I had to try.

"You're going to pay for that, whore," Ian screamed behind me and I heard the shot of his pistol a split second after. The bullet hit the ceiling and plaster rained down on my head. "Next time it won't be the ceiling, Sadie, so I suggest you be a good girl."

"Fuck you! You won't shoot me. You're a coward." I knew I shouldn't taunt him, but I couldn't help it. It felt so damn good.

"Wrong," he said as he aimed the pistol and shot me in the leg, causing me to fall to the floor as I was struck with red-hot searing pain. "That was just to prove that I will shoot you. I hate to destroy your pretty face, because that's the one good thing about you, but I won't hesitate to put the next bullet there if you keep pushing me."

As he leaned down and got in my face, I spat at him. I watched as he wiped the spit from his face and onto his jeans. In the next instant he backhanded me, and I saw stars. I tried to take a few deep breaths to stop the vomit I felt threatening to spill out of my throat but all that did was make the dizziness worse.

Micah, please help me.

That was my last thought before the blackness sucked me in.

∼

My head hurt so bad, but I knew I needed to open my eyes and figure out where I was. I didn't know how long I had been out, but hopefully Ian wasn't around and I could try to get away. As my eyes slowly opened, I took in my surroundings. *Micah's cabin. His bedroom.* As soon as I registered my location, I began to notice other things. Like the fact that there was what felt like rope around both my hands and feet. Like the fact that I was naked. I tried to move my arms and legs and realized I was tied up and spread out on the bed like some sort of human sacrifice. I turned my head towards the door and Ian was standing there with a lazy smile on his face.

"I'm so glad you decided to wake up. This wouldn't have been as much fun otherwise. Now he gets to hear your screams while he watches you suffer," Ian was walking toward me as he spoke.

My phone chose that moment to start ringing and I prayed it was Micah. Ian snatched the phone off the nightstand, looked at the screen and said, "Perfect timing. Biker boy must miss you. I'm gonna answer on speaker phone. Be good and don't spoil my fun."

"He-hello," I stammered as Ian held the phone to my ear.

"Hey, sweetness. I'm about an hour out. How are things at the house?" Micah sounded so happy. I hated that I'd brought this to his home.

"Things are okay, I guess. Um, I'm almost done with the cookies," I mumbled, hoping he'd catch on. I wasn't making cookies. I may be able to cook but baking had never been my strong suit and Micah teased me about it all the time.

"Cookies, I thought—" Micah started before he was cut off by Ian's voice.

"Bitch!" Ian slapped me across the face. Blood dribbled out of the corner of my mouth as I turned my head back toward Ian in time to watch him try to use Facetime.

"Sadie! Sadie, what's going on?" Micah's voice was full of anger.

"Micah," I screamed. "Ian's here."

"Shut up!" Ian yelled just as he got Facetime to work. I was horrified when he turned the phone to run over my prone body so Micah could see what he'd done.

"Oh, baby, I'm on my way. Just hang on a little longer for me, okay?" Micah took a deep breath before he continued. "I swear to God if you hurt her anymore, you'll pray for death. I will make you pay for all the beatings if it's the last thing I do." I'd never heard Micah this furious.

"Oh, I think she can take a little more. Can't you, *sweetness*? And what fun, I have a whole hour to satisfy the beast," Ian taunted and that was when I noticed he had switched his pistol out for a knife. A wicked looking blade with a serrated edge. *He always did have a thing for knives.*

"Don't you fucking dare—" Micah started, but Ian punched the end button on the phone, cutting him off.

"Now, let's see what kind of fun we can have before biker boy gets here. We have a little more time than I anticipated. Where should we start?" Ian was sitting on the side of the bed running the blade of the knife down my cheek. I wanted to fight, but I couldn't. The blood loss from my leg and struggling against the ropes had made me weak.

I squeezed my eyes shut as I felt him move the blade over my breasts and down my stomach.

"Open your eyes! I want you to watch what I do to you."

I squeezed my eyes tighter and felt the point of the knife dig into the bullet wound on my leg. My eyes flew open as I screamed and thrashed my head from side to side and struggled against by bindings.

"That's better. Now, where should I start? Maybe I should start with that pussy of yours since that's what biker boy seems to love about you." Ian dragged the blade up my inner thigh, and it took all of my restraint to resist tensing up. I knew that'd only make it worse. When Ian got to the spot where my thigh ended and my groin started, he dug in, and I felt the blood trickle down my skin. Ian's laugh was hollow, and that scared me even more.

"Or maybe I should slice up your tits? Is biker boy a tit man?" Ian used the serrated edge and sliced across my left breast and then the opposite direction on my right breast. A scream ripped out of me with the pain, but I quickly bit my lip to stop it. Wiping the blade clean on my stomach, Ian tilted his head to the side. "Or maybe, I should just gut you so when he arrives, he'll get to watch you bleed out." And with that, he thrust the blade into my stomach just above my belly button. The pain was so intense, and I bit down harder, a metallic taste coating my mouth. I fought to hold onto consciousness, afraid it was a losing battle.

As I struggled to maintain focus, Ian said, "So beautiful. Will biker boy feel the same? Will he still want to fuck you?" That was the last thing I heard before lights out.

35

MICAH

"Fucking hell!"

I slammed my fist into the steering wheel for the third time. That phone call was the most terrifying thing I had ever experienced, and now, I was stuck at a fucking DUI checkpoint. I'd called the others, but only Jackson answered, and he had still been at work. I had quickly relayed the phone call to him and knew I could trust him to get there as quick as he could. Not quick enough, though.

After what felt like a lifetime, traffic finally started to move, and I made it through the checkpoint without killing anyone. I pressed the gas, not caring if anyone followed me. Bring on the sirens. Part the traffic like Moses parted the fucking Red Sea.

As I got closer to the club, I mentally prepared myself for what I would find when I reached BRB property. When I reached the main house, I threw the Jeep in park and was out the door before the gear shift even settled.

Barreling through the front door, I drew my weapon and methodically began to sweep the first floor. I noted the large puddle of blood just inside the living room and forced my breathing to settle. I had to keep my wits about me if I was going to be worth a damn. As I started up the steps, Griffin and Aiden were coming down, both with guns drawn.

"Where the fuck is she?" I pleaded to both of them.

"I don't know, man. We came home, saw the blood, and started searching. What's going on?" Aiden's voice was laced with steel and Griffin's face was set hard as stone.

"Sadie…I called her, and Ian had her…Oh God, where is she?"

"Did you check your cabin?" Griffin asked.

"Shit!" I turned and raced out the front door with them on my heels. "I'm gonna kill that motherfucker! How did he get in?" We were all running at full speed, not wanting to chance the sound of an engine tipping off the psycho.

When we reached the door, I raised my fist up next to my head, signaling that they stop. Not wanting to waste another second, I motioned them to follow me and we started our sweep. I trusted these men with my life, and once we crossed that threshold, my only thought was to find Sadie and kill that piece of shit.

I ran to my bedroom, and the door was locked. I raised my leg and kicked as hard as I could. Wood splintered and the door flew open. The sight that greeted me had me seeing red. Sadie was tied to the bed, naked and unconscious. Ian was straddling her, hands wrapped around her throat.

"Get the fuck off her!" I commanded as I lunged at him, knocking him off her and onto the floor. I pummeled his face with my fists as hard as I could. Ian tried to block the punches with his arms but failed. Blood was flying out of his nose and I relished the sight.

"Micah! Micah, stop! He's done, man." Aiden came barreling through the door and gripped my arms, trying to pull me off.

"Get off me!" I roared, as I fought to continue my assault. "Let me kill him!"

"No. He isn't worth it. Besides, he's out." Aiden tried to reason with me, but I was still craving vengeance.

"Micah, look at her. Look at Sadie. She needs you." Aiden managed to say the one thing that could make me stop.

As I stood up, I shifted my gaze toward the bed. My stomach plummeted. Sadie had a knife sticking out of her abdomen and there was so much blood. In that moment, I did something that I have never done before. I froze.

"Mic?" Nell's hand rested on my shoulder, and that's when I became aware that the others had arrived.

Jackson placed cuffs on Ian, in case he woke up. *When had he gotten there?* I was dimly aware of Griffin on the phone. To who, I wasn't sure. Nor did I care. My feet carried me to the bed, and I knelt down beside it.

"Sadie...Sadie, can you hear me?" Nothing. "Sweetness, please. Open those pretty blue eyes for me," I pleaded as I ran my hands over her body, assessing her injuries. Her eyes fluttered open and she peered at me through slits.

"Micah," Sadie croaked. Never had anything sounded so beautiful to me.

"Oh, sweetness, hang on. We're gonna get you to a hospital." I turned toward my team. "Call an ambulance. Now!"

"Already done. They're on the way," Griffin responded.

"Brie?" I heard Sadie whisper. I whipped my head around because I wasn't expecting that.

"What about her?" I asked.

"She was...here...Ian...Zach...same person." Sadie's eyes closed as a single tear leaked out.

I heard Nell swear a blue streak behind me.

"On it," Nell said, as she and the others took off to start the hunt.

I turned back to Sadie and started to quickly, but gently,

untie the ropes that bound her. Deep in the recesses of my brain, I knew I should keep talking to her, reassure her, but I was no longer capable of speech.

"Micah?"

"Yeah, baby?" I whispered as my eyes snapped to hers.

"Blanket, please."

"Oh shit. I'm sorry. I wasn't thinking," I mumbled, as I slowly pulled a blanket over her nakedness.

"Thank you," Sadie managed, her teeth chattering. From shock or cold, I wasn't sure.

"I need…I…Micah…"

"Shh, baby. We can talk later, okay?"

Sirens sounded as the ambulance arrived. I brushed my fingers across Sadie's forehead as we waited for the paramedics to come inside. *What is taking them so long?* I wanted to carry her out myself, speed this up a bit, but I was afraid to move her because of the knife.

"No… I need… I tried…," God, I didn't know how long I could listen to her try to speak. "I was… brave." The tears were flowing, and I watched as they silently snaked down her cheeks into her hair.

"Oh, baby. Yes, you were so brave. I'm so proud of you," I said as I brushed my lips over her hair.

Those were our last words before she completely lost consciousness again.

36

GRIFFIN

I had watched Micah pace the damn waiting room at the hospital for the last hour. From what Nell told me, he'd been pacing it for the entire three hours prior to my arrival, too. I had stayed behind with Aiden and Jackson to keep up the search for Brie. Jackson's deputies had taken Ian into custody, and hopefully, the bastard would rot in a cell for the rest of his miserable life.

Jackson had made us leave to be here for Micah and Sadie. And he used some bullshit excuse that we would fuck up any investigation if we stayed. I didn't buy it. He knew we were the best, but he needed to keep up appearances. All I knew was that if the police didn't have anything by morning, my ass was not going to quit. Fuck them! I'd find her. I just hoped I found her alive.

"Micah, come sit down. The doctor will come out as soon as they have something to tell us. Sadie's a fighter. She's going to be fine." I heard Nell try to reassure Micah. It wasn't working, but she tried. That's what mattered.

"I can't sit down. Not when I don't know what's happening. I can't lose her, Nell." Micah responded. I heard the emotion in his voice when he continued. "I just… I love her. I haven't even told her yet and now I might not get a chance to. Shit, why couldn't I say it before? Why'd I wait?"

I heard Nell start to respond, and suddenly, I couldn't stand there and listen any longer, so I strode through the double doors out of the waiting room and walked outside. Staring out at the parking lot, I took a deep breath and felt a hand come down on my shoulder. I swung around, ready to take out the threat and Aiden threw up his hands to block the attack.

"Griffin, Jesus, it's just me."

"Aiden, don't fucking sneak up on me like that." I was angry that I had reacted as I had and knew it wasn't his fault. Luckily, he knew it too and didn't push the matter.

"We'll find her." Aiden's voice was quiet, like he didn't want to put voice to my worry.

"You don't know that. She could be anywhere by now." I heard the fear and took a few deep breaths to calm myself. I couldn't lose Brie, but no one else needed to know that.

"We will. You've got to trust Jackson. He's got a lot of men out searching. They aren't going to quit. And if they do, then we won't. Never leave a man behind. That's what we've always lived by. That didn't stop just because we got out. We'll get her back. You've gotta believe that." Aiden let that all hang in the air between us and said nothing more.

"I'll let Jackson do his thing, but he's got twelve hours. After that, all bets are off." As I turned to go back inside, I said over my shoulder, "Are you coming or what?"

37

MICAH

Taking what felt like the last breath I had, I caught sight of a doctor coming through the doors to the waiting room. She was wearing blue scrubs and there was blood smeared on her shirt. The blood caught me off guard, and then I looked at her face. I was scared by what I saw. She didn't look happy.

"Are you here for Sadie?" She walked right up to me.

"I am. We all are," I responded, sweeping my arm to indicate the entire waiting room. We were the only ones there. Not much happened in our sleepy town that would bring a crowd of this size to the hospital.

"Good. I'm looking for a Micah. Judging by the way you were pacing, I'm assuming that's you." She gave me a once over. "I'm Dr. Burrows. I was the lead surgeon working on Sadie."

"Nice to meet you," I said, shaking her hand. "Yes, I'm Micah. You said she asked for me? So, she's awake? She's okay?" I questioned. Before I could let myself relax, I needed the answers to those questions.

"Yes, she's awake. Why don't you follow me and I'll take

you to her? I can explain everything to the both of you. She wouldn't listen to a word I had to say before I came out and got you," Dr. Burrows said with a small smile. "After I talk to the two of you, then the rest of you can come in two at a time to see her. Visits will have to be kept short. Sadie needs her rest," she said, addressing the rest of my family. Sadie's family.

"Lead the way doc," I instructed. I was getting impatient to see my woman.

Dr. Burrows gave a curt nod before turning to precede me through the double doors and down a long corridor with what I assumed were recovery rooms on either side. We passed three of those rooms before we came to a door, and Dr. Burrows slowed and turned to me before entering.

"Micah, Sadie is a little groggy as the anesthesia is still wearing off, so I'm not sure she's going to be able to comprehend everything I say. I've only given her a low dose of pain medication so she's not as groggy as she could be—"

"Why the hell aren't you giving her stronger pain meds? If she needs them, give them to her," I demanded.

"Micah, please, calm yourself. If you don't, I'm afraid I can't let you go in there. I have to follow my patients wishes, whether I agree or not. Now, can we go in or do you need another minute?"

"Fine. I'm calm. Let's go." I was far from calm, but I wouldn't let her see that. I wanted in that room.

Dr. Burrows turned from me and opened the door. I entered behind her and inhaled sharply at the sight of Sadie lying in the bed. She was so pale and still that, for a second, I was afraid she was dead. She was hooked up to a bunch of monitors, and the beeping noise reminded me she was alive.

Deep breaths. Sadie needs you to be calm.

Walking up to the bed, I picked up Sadie's hand and brought it to my lips. Placing a gentle kiss on her knuckles, I let myself break for a minute before pulling myself together and leaned over her.

"Sweetness? Open those pretty eyes for me. Please," I pleaded.

Sadie's eyes slowly opened, and for a second, I could see the panic in them and the beeping sped up. When her eyes settled on my face, the beeping slowed and she visibly relaxed.

"Micah?" she whispered.

"Yeah, baby. It's me. God, Sadie, you scared me."

Dr. Burrows cleared her throat to remind us she was there, so I stood up and turned to her.

"Okay, doc. Let us have it. What's the damage?" Sadie was a little too out of it to ask questions, so I took the lead.

"Sadie, are you awake enough to hear about your injuries? I want to be sure you know what they are and what the plan moving forward is going to be." Dr. Burrows didn't exclude me, but it was clear that Sadie was her patient.

"I...I think so," Sadie whispered.

"Okay then. For starters, we did an exploratory surgery to determine the extent of the damage to your abdomen. Fortunately, the knife had not been inserted completely, so we were able to see that it had a serrated edge. Knowing that, surgery was the only option to investigate what was going on. We were concerned about internal bleeding and the angle at which the knife had penetrated. Once we extracted the knife, we were able to stop the internal bleeding quickly. Once the bleeding was under control, we noticed that your uterus was slightly enlarged. The tip of the blade missed your uterus by only half an inch, so the swelling concerned us. Using an ultrasound, we were able to determine that the swelling we were seeing was normal for a woman in your condition." Dr. Burrows paused and glanced at both of us before continuing. "Once we were satisfied that we'd done all we could in the abdominal area, we moved our efforts to the gunshot wound on your leg. We cleaned the wound and put a dressing on it. The bullet passed through your calf so while you have a hole where it passed through and a lot of pain, it will heal nicely. We now have you on a low dose pain medication and would like you to stay in the hospital for a few days to be sure that infection doesn't set in and also to monitor your condition to be sure there won't be any complications moving forward."

"You keep saying her 'condition'. What the hell does that mean?" Frustration was running high for me just then. Couldn't she just spit out what she was saying instead of beating around the bush?

"That's a fair question. And by 'condition' I mean that, Sadie, you're pregnant. About eight weeks along. Of course, I'll have an OBGYN check in with you and verify."

"But...wait...did you say I'm pregnant?" Sadie stammered.

"I did. I'm guessing you didn't know?"

"Doc...let me get this straight ...you said...she's pregnant?" I couldn't quite wrap my head around what I was hearing.

"That's exactly what I'm saying," Dr. Burrows smiled as she answered.

"But how...I mean...the baby?" I was afraid to hope that a baby could survive after what Sadie had just been though.

"The baby is just fine. Like I said earlier, an OBGYN will come in to check on both mom and baby, but as long as Sadie rests and takes care of herself, I don't foresee any complications."

"Oh my God. Sadie, did you hear that? You're pregnant. You're going to have a baby. We're going to have a baby." The news finally sank in and I was thrilled.

"I heard. Micah," Sadie voice didn't match my joy. "How did this happen? I'm on the pill." She was crying and my excitement took a backseat to trying to find out what was wrong.

"Baby, what's wrong? This is a good thing. We're going to have a baby. You and me," I said, repeating myself. "This is a good thing."

"It's a great thing," she wailed, "but we didn't plan it. I love you so much and I don't want you to—"

"Stop." I demanded. "What did you say?"

"I said it's a great thing." She looked at me like I'd lost my mind.

"And I agree, but not that. After that." Of course I heard her, but I wanted to hear it again.

"Oh, um, I said I love you." Lowering her eyes, she started to fidget with her hands.

"I love you too, sweetness. So much." Being careful of the IV, I grabbed her hands. "I've loved you for what feels like a lifetime. You are an amazing woman. Beautiful inside and out. I'm so sorry I didn't tell you sooner. Never again. I will tell you every day for as long as you'll let me that I love you."

"You love me?" Sadie cried.

"So damn much. Sweetness, please stop crying. I can't stand to watch you cry."

"Oh, Micah. I'm crying because I'm happy. I thought it was all one sided. I love you more than I ever thought possible. And I know we're doing this all backwards, but I'm so glad I'm having your baby. Our baby. He's going to have the best of both of us and I can't wait."

"He?" I teased. "I want a little girl with fiery red hair just like her mama."

"And I want a boy who's as amazing as his father."

"Marry me? I don't want to waste any more time. I want you to be my wife. You're already my best friend, my lover, the mother of my child." Placing my hand on her belly, I realized that the doctor was still in the room and this wasn't the most romantic declaration of love or proposal, but I couldn't wait.

"Are you sure? I mean, I want to marry you, but this is so fast. You need to be sure. When I get married again, it will be for life, no matter what." Uncertainty crossed her features and I made a silent vow to myself to make sure that she never felt uncertain again.

"I've never been more sure of anything else in my life. I want to spend forever with you. So, what do you say? Will you marry me?"

"Yes. Oh yes, I'll marry you," Sadie cried. I wrapped her up in my arms as carefully as possible. Then I heard applause behind me. Laughing, I stood up and turned around. Our family was standing just inside the door. Some were crying, some were laughing, and they were all clapping.

"I couldn't resist. It seemed like a moment to share with family and not a surgeon you just met." Dr. Burrows laughed as she wiped tears from her own cheeks. "I'll give you all ten minutes to quietly celebrate. Sadie is still recovering after all. Then I'm throwing the lot of you out."

"I'm staying," I growled. No way was she kicking me out. I was here for the long haul.

"Of course, Micah. You can stay, but the rest of you," she turned to everyone else, "will have to leave. No arguments."

"You got it, doc."

"We'll go."

"No problem."

Everyone talked at once, but I tuned them out.

"I love you," I said, looking down at the woman who had survived hell and come out the other side…to me.

EPILOGUE

SADIE

I felt as big as an elephant. Micah hated it when I said that, but I was nine months pregnant and *huge*. We had found out pretty early on in the pregnancy that not only were we having a little boy, but we were also having a little girl. Twins! I still couldn't believe it. When the doctor showed us those two little spots on the ultrasound and explained what we were looking at, I thought Micah was going to pass out. We were both shocked, to say the least, but we couldn't be happier.

We decided to wait to get married until after the babies were born. When we made that decision, we thought we would have Brie back, but still no luck. I felt responsible for her disappearance, even though everyone assured me it wasn't my fault. Sometimes it was easier to believe that than others. The hardest times were when I was around Griffin. He had been single-minded when it came to finding Brie. He would be gone for days at a time searching. One time, he was gone for a month. Micah tried to keep some of the details from me, saying I didn't need the stress because it wasn't good for the babies, but he couldn't keep everything from me. I could tell when he was lying, so he quit trying. I loved him for trying, but I loved him more for including me.

Ian was still sitting in a jail cell, awaiting trial. I wasn't worried about him getting out. They had him on kidnapping, assault with a deadly weapon and attempted murder. He'd be locked up for a long while.

While in jail, all of Ian's phone calls were being monitored. Jackson was hoping that he had a partner or something. I wasn't sure what I hoped. Ian having a partner meant that there was a chance Brie was still alive, but the thought of other dangerous people out there like Ian, or worse, petrified me. So far, the phone calls hadn't panned out, but everyone was still hopeful.

Enough!

This was my time…mine and Micah's. I tried for a long time to find reason behind Ian's abuse and the attack that night but knew that I would never find one. At least not one that made sense to a sane person.

"Hey, mama. How are those babies of mine?" Micah's arms wrapped around me. Well, as far around me as they could.

"They want out, Micah. Make them come out." We were still in bed. I'd been sleeping in a lot lately, and Micah let me. In fact, he usually insisted on it.

"Any day mama," he chuckled.

"Today would be good," I grumbled.

Micah continued to chuckle. It was wonderful to hear him so carefree. It didn't happen often, especially with Brie still missing. It had certainly been a stressful few months. We had finished construction on the additional housing for future clients. We had two of the units occupied now, and I knew that it was taking a toll on Micah. Being president of the BRB and taking care of me was a lot. Not to mention everything else. But he was great at it and never complained.

Suddenly, I felt a sharp pain and something wet between my legs.

"Um, Micah…"

"Yeah, sweetness?" His breath was right at my ear.

"We need names. Like, now."

"Okay. I thought we'd agreed on Isaiah and Isabelle?"

"Um, okay. Well, I think Isaiah and Isabelle are ready." Trying to sit up, I felt Micah's arms come under me to give me leverage.

"I know you want them to come out, Sadie, but you can't—"

"Micah," I shouted to cut him off. "They're coming. Now. My water just broke."

"Oh, shit. Okay. Um—" My screaming from a contraction cut him off. "Breathe, baby." He pulled out his cell phone and called the hospital to let them know we'd be on our way.

The pain from the contraction eased, and I looked at Micah and said, "You ready, daddy?"

"So ready," he said with a huge grin on his face.

~

Micah

Isabella was born first, with Isaiah entering the world five minutes later. They were both perfect. Isaiah had his mother's red hair while Isabella's was a little lighter. Both had blue eyes like their mother. We'd been at the hospital for two days, and Sadie and the babies would be released today. I had realized when we were buying car seats two months ago that Rhiannon wasn't going to cut it, so Sadie and I bought our own Jeep so we weren't constantly taking the one the BRB shared.

Everyone was at the main house waiting for us to get

home. *Almost everyone.* Sadie was feeding Isaiah while I held Isabella and we waited for the doctor to bring the release papers, and the sight of our baby at her breast was incredible.

"Look at them, Micah," Sadie whispered.

"I see them, mama. They're perfect. Just like you." I smiled at her.

"We're going to have our hands full," she laughed, "but you're right. They're perfect."

Just then the doctor came in, and within minutes, we were on our way out of the room and loading the Jeep to take our babies home. Sadie sat in the back between the car seats. As I drove, I constantly looked in the rear-view mirror. I couldn't stop looking.

Within twenty minutes, we were pulling into the driveway and parking. Before getting out of the car, I turned in my seat to look at my family. I heard the door to the main house open and everyone was hollering for us to come inside. I ignored them for a few minutes and simply stared.

"What?" Sadie asked, pushing a lock of her hair behind her ear. Her gaze went from me, to Isaiah, and then to Isabelle, before coming back to me.

"Thank you," I whispered around the tears clogging my throat.

"For what?"

"Everything. For giving me everything."

BONUS CHAPTER

Need more of Micah and Sadie? Sign up for my newsletter at andirhodes.com for an EXCLUSIVE bonus chapter, as well as updates on upcoming novels and giveaways.

SNEAK PEEK AT BROKEN INNOCENCE

BOOK TWO IN THE BROKEN REBEL BROTHERHOOD SERIES

Griffin...
I loved her for years but she never loved me back.
When she was taken, I snapped.
Now she's back and not herself.
She's an empty shell of the woman I knew.
But I still love her.
Her demons are many, and I want to slay every one.
Problem is, she thinks she's too broken.

Brie...
He never knew I loved him. I made sure of that.
Then I was taken and made unloveable.
My past hadn't prepared me for the hell I was put through.
I'd wanted to die, but he wouldn't let me.
No matter what I did, he made sure to save me.
He says he loves me and that he always will.
Problem is, I'm too broken to love him back.

Broken Innocence is a complete story with a guaranteed HEA. This book contains subject matter that some may find disturbing. Reader discretion is advised.

PROLOGUE

BRIE

Thump thump... thump thump... thump thump...

My heartbeat echoed in my ears as consciousness seeped in. Humid air permeated my lungs, carrying traces of dirt with it. Confusion clouded my brain when I registered a musty smell. Something wasn't right. I was supposed to be at a barbecue, surrounded by my friends, not curled up on a dirt floor with a throbbing headache.

Dry soil sifted through my fingers as I leveraged myself up on shaky arms, wincing as tiny pebbles dug into my palms. My body felt as if something were weighing me down, but there was nothing. There was a shred of light that was swallowed up by surrounding darkness, and I had to blink several times before my eyes adjusted to the single flickering bulb swinging above me on a string.

My last memory flickered through my mind like a movie reel, and I felt as if I'd been sucker-punched.

Sadie's face draining of color... The butt of the gun crashing against my temple...

Zach had done this.

I realized the error in my thinking and shook my head to clear the cobwebs. Not Zach...Ian.

"Where the fuck am I?" My voice echoed in the cavernous space around me.

As a Veteran, I had the training to size up any situation, both quickly and accurately, but I wasn't firing on all cylinders. My thoughts were groggy and my movements sluggish, as if some sort of drug was coursing through my system.

"I thought you'd never wake up." A deep voice sounded from the shadows and adrenaline surged through my veins. I whipped around toward the sound and pain shot through me from my toes on up, causing me to immediately regret the movement.

Don't let them see your fear. The voice in my head was a mantra from my military days.

"Who the hell are you?" I demanded of the unfamiliar figure now standing before me. I let my gaze travel up and down his gangly body, trying to determine if I'd ever seen him before.

Nope.

Green eyes stared back at me, but I couldn't tell if they were really *seeing* me. They looked a bit maniacal. *I'd remember those eyes.*

"I wasn't sure how much etorphine to inject. I'm glad to see it didn't kill you." The way he smiled as he said that scared me more than I cared to admit. I'd seen smiles like that before. It was the smile of someone who thought causing pain was like a Sunday stroll through the park.

"I'm Steve, by the way," he said as he extended his hand to shake mine. *Yeah, right!*

"Steve?" That seemed like such a normal name. A *nice* name.

No reply. *Okay, moving on.* I scratched my head as a million questions flooded my mind.

"Etorphine?" It was the first question I could put voice to. Of course, I had more, but I was too afraid of the answers, so I held them in. For now.

"Well, pretty," I cringed at the term, "Ian would have a fit if I killed you, but he doesn't mind if I play a little." Steve laughed and it sounded like pure evil.

"But… how… why…?" I stammered, hating myself for the small display of emotion.

"Because." He started pacing back and forth. He appeared agitated now, so I let him work out whatever problem was going on in that crazy mind of his. "Ian called and told me he had a problem." The pacing stopped and Steve stood only a foot away, coldly staring at my tits. "A pretty problem."

My fist shot out, connecting with his jaw. His neck snapped back, reminding me of a bobble-head, and the sound of bone breaking fueled my rage. I continued to pummel his face and reveled in the blood that sprayed from his nose. Steve tried to block my attack by throwing up his arms, but he couldn't keep up with my adrenaline induced energy.

As much fun as it was to take my anger and fear out on him, my knuckles were bruised and bleeding and my body started to slow down. Before I knew it, I had no fight left in me.

"Fuck you, asshole." I spat at Steve's prone body, now lying in the dirt.

Dizziness washed over me and I swayed. I'd pushed myself too far. My ass hit the ground and I fell to my back, holding my head in my hands. I needed to get my wits about me if I wanted to get out of this hell. Steve groaned and I managed to lift my head and ascertain that he was still lying there, bloody. The fact that he was able to manage any sound at all told me just how little time I had to escape. Men like him fell, but rarely did they stay down as long as you hoped.

I rolled to my stomach and forced myself up to my knees, ignoring the tilt-a-whirl feeling. After assuring myself I wasn't going to end up on my ass again, I stood, resting my hands on my thighs. My lungs burned from the exertion of the fight and it took me several more minutes before I felt confident in my ability to actually put one foot in front of the other.

The door was across the room, if one could call it that, and when I reached it, I twisted the knob. I didn't really think it would open, but I had to try. I pounded against the barrier and yelled out, praying that someone, anyone, would hear me. My arms tired quickly, still overworked from beating Steve, and I let them fall to my sides. Defeat wasn't an option, but I had to face the fact that the easy way out wasn't going to be *my* way out.

"Okay, what would *he* do?" Talking out loud, I ran through our Survival, Evasion, Resistance, and Escape training. It had saved my ass before and it would now. "First, I need to—"

Pain shot through my skull as I was dragged away from the door by my hair. I reached back to grab the source of my agony and ease the burn in my scalp, but came up empty. I dug my heels in, trying to stop from being dragged farther from freedom and only managed to slow it down a little.

"Motherfucker!" If physical action wouldn't work, maybe name-calling would.

Get real, Brie. You're only going to antagonize him.

Steve was now standing with his legs braced apart on either side of my hips. He stared down at me, blood trickling from his nose.

"Don't ever do that again!" Steve screamed, sounding more commanding than I gave him credit for. He wiped the crimson from his face with the back of his hand, only managing to smear it across his cheeks to his hairline.

"Do what?" I countered, trying to sit up.

Shut up, Brie!

His face contorted with rage just before his boot connected with my chest and I flew back, hitting my head on the dirt floor. Stars sparkled behind my eyelids, and I fought to maintain consciousness. Even though passing out was not an option, I kept my eyes closed, in hopes that he'd back off, even if for a minute or two.

When he didn't kick me again, I took a chance and opened my eyes to slits. Steve was pacing back and forth, muttering incoherently. When he turned back to look at me, I squeezed my eyes shut.

"Why did you make me do that?" He was close. Too close. But he didn't sound as crazed as he had a few minutes before.

I ignored his question and peered up at him. We stared at each other, both silent, but both speaking volumes with our glares.

He started pacing again, and I tracked his every movement. The longer he paced, the calmer he appeared.

"I had to bring you here. Ian will understand. He'll see. I'm doing this for him." Steve wasn't talking to me, but rather to whoever, or whatever, was in his head with him.

"Doing what for him?"

I wasn't entirely sure I wanted the answer.

I watched as he went to the door and bent over to pick something up. I tracked his every move as he pulled a Ziploc bag out of a camouflage backpack and threw it at me. I glanced down as it sent dust clouds billowing, and I struggled to stop the coughing fit it elicited. Once I had my hacking under control, I squinted to see what was in the bag and had to school my expression. *Food.* At least I'd be able to eat. Build up my strength. I'd bide my time, strategize, plan. I was good at that. And then I'd get the fuck out.

"Eat up."

"I'm not hungry," I lied. My stomach chose that moment to growl, filling the space with its intensity.

"Fine," he snickered. *Bastard.*

As I watched him leave, I listened for the telltale signs of a lock. The sharp clank of metal echoed in the space, and I let myself relax a little, sighing as some of the tension left my body. I picked up the bag he had tossed, opened it and sniffed its contents. Beef Jerky. As I pulled a piece out and brought it to my lips, a shiver raced through me and my thoughts spiraled out of control.

How long had I been gone? Has the BRB noticed I'm missing? Will they find me? Are they even looking for me?

"Of course they are." I ate the rest of the meager offering and berated myself for such thoughts.

If anyone could find me, it was *him*.

ABOUT THE AUTHOR

Andi Rhodes is an author whose passion is creating romance from chaos in all her books! She writes MC (motorcycle club) romance with a generous helping of suspense and doesn't shy away from the more difficult topics. Her books can be triggering for some so consider yourself warned. Andi also ensures each book ends with the couple getting their HEA! Most importantly, Andi is living her real life HEA with her husband and their boxers.

For access to release info, updates, and exclusive content, be sure to sign up for Andi's newsletter at andirhodes.com.

ALSO BY ANDI RHODES

Broken Rebel Brotherhood

Broken Souls

Broken Innocence

Broken Boundaries

Broken Rebel Brotherhood: Complete Series Box set

Broken Rebel Brotherhood: Next Generation

Broken Hearts

Broken Wings

Broken Mind

Bastards and Badges

Stark Revenge

Slade's Fall

Jett's Guard

Soulless Kings MC

Fender

Joker

Piston

Greaser

Riker

Trainwreck

Squirrel

Gibson

Satan's Legacy MC

Snow's Angel

Toga's Demons

Magic's Torment

Printed in Great Britain
by Amazon